Lincoln's gaze snapped to Josi's office window. She wasn't there.

He'd been sure she would be watching, relaying the details to a dispatcher by phone. Maybe even looking for him.

He turned in a slow circle, hoping she hadn't wandered into the chaos where she would be vulnerable to attack. Then, suddenly, he understood.

The gunfire wasn't intended to cause harm. Each shot had done exactly what it was meant to do. And Lincoln had reacted precisely as expected.

He'd left Josi alone.

He was in motion before the thought had finished forming.

His chest ached with effort as he leaped over abandoned bags and toppled strollers on his way to the stable. He sucked in his first full breath of hope as a familiar figure came into view outside Josi's office.

"Mama!" He slowed upon approach. "You okay?"

She nodded, eyes wide and expression aghast. "I am. I saw you in the field, and I came to check on Josi."

Lincoln froze beside his mother, gaze fixed on the empty office before them.

Josi was gone.

UNDER SIEGE

JULIE ANNE LINDSEY

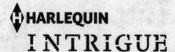

HARLEQUIN

INTRIGUE

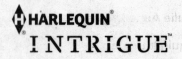

HARLEQUIN®
INTRIGUE™

Recycling programs
for this product may
not exist in your area.

ISBN-13: 978-1-335-59165-4

Under Siege

Copyright © 2024 by Julie Anne Lindsey

For questions and comments about the quality of this book, please contact us
at CustomerService@Harlequin.com.

TM and ® are trademarks of Harlequin Enterprises ULC.

Harlequin Enterprises ULC
22 Adelaide St. West, 41st Floor
Toronto, Ontario M5H 4E3, Canada
www.Harlequin.com

Printed in Lithuania

MIX
Paper | Supporting
responsible forestry
FSC® C021394

Julie Anne Lindsey is an obsessive reader who was once torn between the love of her two favorite genres: toe-curling romance and chew-your-nails suspense. Now she gets to write both for Harlequin Intrigue. When she's not creating new worlds, Julie can be found carpooling her three kids around northeastern Ohio and plotting with her shamelessly enabling friends. Winner of the Daphne du Maurier Award for Excellence in Mystery/Suspense, Julie is a member of International Thriller Writers, Romance Writers of America and Sisters in Crime. Learn more about Julie and her books at julieannelindsey.com.

Books by Julie Anne Lindsey

Harlequin Intrigue

Beaumont Brothers Justice

Closing In On Clues
Always Watching
Innocent Witness
Under Siege

Heartland Heroes

SVU Surveillance
Protecting His Witness
Kentucky Crime Ring
Stay Hidden
Accidental Witness
To Catch a Killer

Visit the Author Profile page at Harlequin.com.

CAST OF CHARACTERS

Josi Roberts—Stable manager at the Beaumont Ranch, Josi was a former troubled youth taken in by the family and is now searching for a missing friend.

Lincoln Beaumont—A former military hero and current stable hand at his family's ranch, Lincoln is working hard to assist local law enforcement in the safe recovery and return of the missing Tara Stone. Secretly in love with his boss, Josi Roberts, he'll stop at nothing to protect her and return her friend to safety.

Detective Finn Beaumont—A Marshal's Bluff detective, and brother to Lincoln, Finn is investigating the disappearance of Tara Stone and the possibility of a revived illegal fight club.

Tara Stone—Missing woman and friend of Josi. Tara's brother died in the ring of an illegal fight club that was shut down for a while but is up and running once more.

Marcus Stone—The former love of Josi's life, and Tara's older brother, Marcus lost his life three years ago at an illegal fight club.

Mrs. Beaumont—The Beaumont family matriarch runs a restorative ranch with her husband and champions the interests of her five grown sons.

Chapter One

Josi Roberts ran a hand along the side of her favorite stallion, Lancelot, proud of the big guy for his incredible patience. "You did good this afternoon," she told him. "You made a whole lot of kids smile."

The autumn afternoon had been bright and sunny, showcasing a cloudless blue sky with only a slight nip in the air. Evening, however, had come with rain. Thanks to a tropical storm off the coast of Florida, things would get worse before they got better in Marshal's Bluff, North Carolina, Josi's beloved hometown. Scattered showers and frigid gusts were predicted to continue until dawn, maybe through the weekend. That was all fine by her. She found the pattering on the stable roof and drops on her office windowpane soothing. After a long day of hard work, the breeze blowing through the open barn doors was more than welcome.

Lancelot lowered his big nose to her head and nuzzled, filling her heart impossibly further. His dark brown mane was a stark contrast to her blond, sun-bleached locks, as was his regal size. At five foot four, Josi fit easily beneath his chin, with plenty of room for a ten-gallon hat or two. He nibbled mischievously at the oversize cotton scrunchie holding the hair away from her face, and she laughed.

"Hey, now." Josi pulled back, checking to be sure he

hadn't stolen her hair tie again. "They should've named you Mischief."

He watched her with keen, all-seeing eyes as she smiled at his handsome face.

"Just one more open house event next week," she promised. "Then this place won't be so overrun for a while. You and I will both get a break."

Lancelot snorted and swished his tail, glad for the attention. Probably because he knew he was her favorite.

"Show-off," she whispered, rubbing a palm along his cheek. She made a mental note to give the other horses in her care some extra love, lest they feel slighted and unhappy.

The Beaumont Ranch, where she lived and worked, opened its doors publicly every fall in a series of preplanned Community Days events. Today's schedule, and next week's, featured the horses. Ranch hands gave introductory workshops on equine care and maintenance as well as beginners' riding lessons. People of influence and affluence in the community made appearances to donate money and raise awareness. Others came because a young person they loved needed help, likely a total life reset. Many visited because this had once been their home, where they'd reached a turning point and been given a fresh start. Those folks usually just wanted to squeeze the people who'd given them the love and time they'd needed to sort themselves out.

Josi would be one of the latter someday, she supposed, though she couldn't imagine ever leaving the ranch. She wasn't a member of the Beaumont family by blood, but they'd taken her in when she'd needed help most. At eighteen, she'd spent most of her life in foster care while her mom had repeatedly tried to clean herself up and failed. Josi had been aging out of the system fast, and no one had wanted to take in a kid who was nearly grown. Especially one so well known for rebelling over the short straw she'd drawn in life.

Somehow, none of that had fazed Mr. and Mrs. Beaumont. Instead, they'd insisted they saw promise in her, and they gave her hope—something she hadn't felt in a very long time. They'd also given her a safe place to stay, good food and thoughtful counsel on her options for the future. Then they'd offered her a job at the stables to earn some money before her birthday. Now, five years later, she still lived on the property, as the stable's manager, with no thought of going anywhere else.

Some days it overwhelmed her heart and soul to belong to a place like this and people like these. Most of the other foster kids she'd spent her rowdy teen years with had to figure things out on their own. Some joined the military. A few turned to crime or drugs. Plenty were getting by now, but it hadn't been easy, and the paths they'd taken had been hard. She was one of the lucky ones and she thought about that fact every day.

Josi grabbed the broom leaning against the wall and returned to sweeping errant bits of hay and dirt from the textured concrete floor. The cell phone in her back pocket vibrated as she worked, and she paused to pull it from her jeans.

The name on the screen surprised her. She hadn't heard from Tara Stone, the younger sister of Josi's one teenage love, in ages. They hadn't spoken on any sort of regular basis since Tara's biological brother had died a few years back, and Josi attended the funeral. A pang of guilt hit her chest. Josi and Tara had been close once. She'd loved Tara's brother, as much as anyone who'd never been loved could anyway. But Josi had checked out of their lives before Marcus died, and she'd kept her distance afterward to protect her own pulverized heart. It was selfish and not something Josi would do today, but she'd still been healing from old wounds then. Today, however, she was prepared and willing to help anyone, however she could.

Josi answered the call on a long inhale, hoping Tara wanted to share good news instead of bad. They'd lost a couple of friends from their old circle for heartbreaking reasons in recent years, and she hated to think of losing another.

"Hey, Tara, what's up?"

"Josi..." Her friend's voice was shaky and thin. Her raspy breaths gave the impression she'd been crying. "I know it's been a while, and I've got no business calling you for this, but I need a favor. I can't think of anyone else it's safe to call."

Josi's muscles tensed. "What do you need?"

"A ride. Now."

Something in the broken cadence of Tara's words set Josi's feet in motion. "Are you at home?" she asked, already slipping into her office to power down the computer and grab her keys. She wasn't even sure if Tara still lived in the same place as before. She'd shared that rental with Marcus.

"No. I'm at the Bayside Motel on Route Nine." Tara sniffed. "I made a mistake coming here, but my truck won't start, and I want to go home."

"Of course," Josi said, relieved to know exactly where Tara was and how to get there. "Are you in danger? Should I call the police first? Or are you going to be okay for about twenty-five minutes?"

A long pause stretched across the line as Josi flipped the light switch and locked the door.

"I think I trusted the wrong guy."

"Relatable," Josi said, hoping to lighten the moment. "Just hurry."

The call ended, and Josi turned the phone around to frown at it. Nothing good ever happened at the motel where Tara was waiting for rescue, and if she was calling Josi for a ride after all this time, the situation must be bad. She couldn't help wondering whom Tara had trusted and why that had been a mistake. Did Josi know him? Had he hurt her friend?

The clatter of a falling feed bucket nearly sent Josi out of her skin. She pressed a palm to her chest as she spun in the direction of the sound.

Lincoln Beaumont, the grumpiest, and arguably the sexiest, of five excellent-looking brothers stared back.

"Goodness!" She huffed a shaky breath, struggling to calm her frantically beating heart.

He raised his eyebrows at her over-the-top response. "Everything all right?" he asked.

The gentle lilt of his Southern drawl was sweet as honey on his tongue, and the image that thought conjured left Josi speechless. He bent to swipe the fallen bucket from the ground, curious eyes narrowing when he straightened. Lincoln had been in the military when Josi came to stay at the ranch, still young and scared. Now, she was his boss, and he was slowly stealing her heart. Not that he had a clue.

After two years of working together, the attraction she'd felt upon their first official introduction had grown steadily from a hopeless crush to something more. His moss-green eyes and barely-there smile were the sexiest of icings on the sweetest possible cake. He hid his big, squishy, teddy-bear heart behind terse words and sharp tones, but she knew the truth. She saw it every day, and she was hopelessly lost because of that knowledge. Now, there was only one man for her, and he'd never know it was him.

She'd been out on a date or two in the last year, but Lincoln had silently set the bar too high. No other man would ever measure up.

Lincoln never dated. Most people couldn't seem to see past his grouchy facade, when all they had to do was look. But most folks were just too busy.

"Jos?" he asked, snapping her back to the moment.

"I'm fine." She shook off the silly, lovestruck thoughts and passed him on the newly swept floor. "I've got to run an errand. Can you lock the stable when you head out?"

"Sure, but I just finished up. You need a hand with anything?"

Her steps faltered for a moment, and she turned to stare. Lincoln had never offered to tag along with her on trips outside the ranch. And she'd never known him to drop anything, now that she thought about it. Her gaze slid to the empty feed bucket, secure in his hands. Lincoln was methodical and a near recluse. So what was he up to?

He waited, unspeaking and brow furrowed. His down-turned mouth told her to walk away.

Yet he'd offered to come.

She shook her head. She was wasting time. Tara had asked her to hurry and debating the merits of an evening ride with Lincoln Beaumont wasn't doing her friend any favors. "No. I've got it, thanks."

He worked his jaw, scrutinizing her.

Josi lifted one hand in a quick hip-high wave, then turned and jogged through the stable, into the night.

TWENTY-THREE MINUTES LATER, Josi piloted her hatchback into the nearly empty parking lot outside the Bayside Motel.

The rain had steadily increased as she drove, forming puddles along the roadside and forcing her wipers to work overtime. She motored past the square detached office to the large, L-shaped structure beyond. Two stories of exposed red doors faced her, each with a rusty number above a peephole, a large window next to each door and the curtains drawn on all but one.

Arriving at the motel after dark incited the worst kind of nostalgia. Josi had spent her share of time in the outdated, barely cleaned rooms, usually attending parties while the hotel manager looked the other way. The place was known for renting by the hour and a number of other practices that made it the perfect place for anyone wanting to meet privately and without a record of their time. Guests paying with cash weren't asked any questions.

She shuddered at the memories of her teen and adolescent years, and thanked her lucky stars she'd taken a different path into adulthood. She hoped Tara had too, and that her presence here tonight was an anomaly, not a norm.

She shifted into Park along the far edge of the lot, beneath the only working streetlight, and surveyed the situation. Last she'd seen her, Tara owned a rusty pickup truck significantly older than herself, but she had no idea what Tara drove these days. Josi supposed it could be any of the vehicles scattered throughout the dark lot. At least her friend would be able to see her clearly in the cone of light, despite the storm.

A flickering neon sign high overhead announced vacancies, but more than half of the security lights were out. An ice machine sat beside an outdoor picnic area and dilapidated iron grill. The pool was empty, its belly covered in fallen leaves, trash and dirt.

Josi sent a text to Tara, letting her know she'd arrived.

Then she sent a follow-up asking for her room number. If she knew where Tara was, she could park closer and not have to cross the creepy lot alone while getting soaked. The thought sent goose bumps over Josi's skin. She turned a knob on her dashboard, circulating heat throughout the car.

Movement drew her eyes back to the room with the open curtains. The blue light of a television flashed against a visible wall. Two shadows appeared, then vanished in swift succession.

A nervous chill rocked down Josi's spine, and she checked her surroundings to be sure she was alone. Sheets of rain, along with the growing darkness, obscured her view and increased her anxiety. That Tara hadn't responded to her text only made matters worse.

Her friend's quaking voice came back to mind as Josi sent another text. It'd been nearly thirty minutes since they'd spoken. What if whatever Tara had been afraid of happening already occurred? What if Josi was too late?

She tapped her fingers against the back of the phone, waiting for a response, wondering if it was too soon to call the police.

A hotel door swung open across the lot, and Tara ran out. She scanned the space, her attention seeming to settle on Josi's SUV, then she darted away, moving quickly in the opposite direction.

"Hey!" Josi called, unfastening her seat belt and climbing into the storm. "Hey! Tara!" She waved her arms as the first clap of thunder split the air. Maybe she hadn't seen Josi after all, or her friend hadn't recognized her.

A second figure emerged from the room, and a flash of light on the heels of a second, more unnatural, boom ripped a scream from Josi's throat. *Gunfire.*

She stumbled back, bumping into her open car door, eyes

searching the night for Tara. She was trying to understand what was happening, and how it could be real.

But Tara had vanished.

The gunman turned on Josi, illuminated in the street-light. He extended his arm, weapon in hand, as he strode determinedly through the puddled lot in her direction.

Her phone buzzed as she scrambled back into her SUV. A single-word message from Tara lit the screen.

Run

Josi jerked the shifter into Drive. She jammed her foot against the gas pedal, spinning her vehicle in a wild half donut. She fishtailed on the wet asphalt as her tires searched for purchase, then she peeled away.

A second shot went off behind her as she swerved onto the main road, sending her cell phone onto the passenger-side floorboards. She didn't stop or look back until the Bayside Motel disappeared from her rearview mirror.

Chapter Two

Lincoln took his time after dinner with his family, lingering to help with dishes and cleanup, but keeping one eye fixed on the long gravel driveway outside the kitchen window. The Beaumonts shared dinner most weeknights and breakfast quite often as well. Even his brothers, who lived elsewhere, were known to show up for several meals a week. Whatever else was going on in any of their lives, family came first, and sitting together over food was a good way to keep the lines of communication open and flowing. Their mama had taught them that. Everyone was busy these days, but they all needed to eat, so why not break bread together?

His parents put a heavy emphasis on building strong, healthy relationships. Which meant making time for, and giving regular attention to, the people who were important to them. They'd also taught Lincoln and his brothers to engage in regular conversations, to listen more than they spoke and never to put off the occasionally necessary maintenance when cracks formed in the foundation. He was sure those lessons had made it possible for his family to grow stronger over the years and to become larger as his brothers had fallen in love, gotten married and had children of their own. Beaumonts didn't start new lives somewhere else with their spouses—they formed new branches on the ever-expanding tree.

Lincoln hadn't been much of a conversationalist for the last couple of years, but he showed up every night, and he listened. He helped when he could.

Lately he'd especially enjoyed seeing Josi at the table, her bright smile and deep dimples popping out with each bout of laughter. His family clearly viewed her as kin, and she'd accepted them wholly, long before he'd grown so attached.

Her absence tonight, coupled with the hasty way she'd left the stable earlier, had stolen his appetite. The increasing winds and sheeting rain felt like an extension of his inner distress. Maybe it was intuition. Maybe it was post-traumatic-stress-induced fear. Either way, he couldn't shake the bone-deep sensation that something was wrong.

"Lincoln," his mom said softly, a moment before moving into his peripheral vision.

He dipped his chin without making eye contact, attention fixed on the world outside.

She set a soft hand on his shoulder, as was her routine now. She'd devised the pattern following his return from the military. After 74 days spent in captivity, the honorable discharge had been a kindness. In truth, he'd become useless to the army, to his men and to himself. He'd needed time to heal, so he'd come home. And more than two years later, his mother still announced her approach and waited for his acknowledgment before touching him.

He appreciated the lengths she'd gone to in making him comfortable, but the routine wasn't necessary anymore. Not that it ever had been. In truth, the trauma seemed to have heightened his senses, making him hyperaware of his surroundings. Very few people came within ten feet of him without his knowledge.

Lincoln finished drying the plate in his hands then set it on the stack of others. "Hey, Mama." He lifted one palm to cover hers on his shoulder.

"Everything okay?" she asked. "You barely touched your dinner."

He turned to rest his hip against the big farmhouse sink, breaking their physical connection in favor of a better look at her. The threads of white in her otherwise brown hair seemed to have doubled in the past year or so. The lines around her eyes and mouth had deepened. The idea that things could've gone very differently for him overseas, that he could've missed her growing older, his nieces and nephews being born and growing up, hit like a sledgehammer to his chest. "Everything was delicious."

"Something on your mind then?" she asked, examining him with keen blue eyes.

His traitorous gaze flickered to Josi's empty seat, and he snapped it away quickly. "It's probably nothing."

"If you say so." She surveyed the cleared table. "I wonder what happened to Josi tonight."

He nearly huffed out a laugh at her casual tone and innocent expression.

His mother liked to pretend he and his brothers volunteered information, but she knew and saw everything. She just gave them the courtesy of confirmation.

"I can't say."

"Hmm. When I saw her outside the stable earlier, she was looking forward to rehashing the day over dinner. We were going to make plans for improvements on next week's event."

Lincoln's brother, Austin, appeared with their father in the archway to the family room. Austin slid into his jacket and moseyed in their direction, stopping to kiss their mother's cheek. "I saw Josi heading out as I was coming in," he said. "About an hour before dinner."

Lincoln crossed his arms. "There's nothing wrong with your hearing."

Austin grinned. "You know I hate to be left out of a conversation."

Their dad followed Austin into the kitchen. "We caught the tail end of what you were saying. That's all."

Their mama looked from one son to the other. "It isn't like her to miss a meal without an explanation. I tell her she doesn't have to keep us posted the way she does, but she insists it's a respect issue, never wanting us to worry, or to make her a plate if she knows she won't be here. Did she say anything to you, Lincoln?"

Three sets of curious eyes turned to him.

He shrugged, hoping to look more at ease than he felt, and praying the cold fingers of dread that had curled around his lungs were unfounded. "She got a call and went to run an errand."

Josi had seemed distressed by whatever was said on the other end of the line. He'd heard it in her tone and sensed it in the air halfway across the stable. He'd spontaneously offered to go with her, just in case there was trouble, and she'd looked at him as if he'd grown a second head. Clearly not an offer she was interested in, one he should probably apologize for later. Inviting himself along wasn't exactly good manners.

"What kind of errand?" his mom asked.

Lincoln shook his head. "Didn't say."

Austin examined him, probably seeing everything Lincoln didn't want to show. "If you knew that, then why're you so tense?"

"I'm always tense."

"Not like this," Austin said. "You think something could be wrong? Or is it just because——" He slid his eyes toward their mama before returning his cool gaze to Lincoln. "You know." *Because it's her*, the look seemed to say.

Lincoln fought the urge to rub the back of his neck. Fidgeting would give him away. Instead, he stared, careful to control his expression.

The Beaumonts were a military family. Everyone had served, including their mother. His brothers had all taken up careers involving surveillance and protection. Two PIs, one detective and an ATF officer. His parents ran a ranch where seeing through troubled teens' problems and into their hearts was a specialty.

Secrets weren't easily kept on the ranch.

Lincoln pushed away from the sink. "I'm sure nothing's wrong. Josi's with a friend, and I'm tired. A whole lot of folks came through this place today, and y'all know how I feel about people." He kissed his mom's cheek, clapped Austin on the back, then nodded to his dad. "I'm going to head out." He retrieved his coat and hat from hooks near the front door.

He made it as far as the porch, still threading his arms into coat sleeves, before his mother called out. "When you see Josi come in, let her know we missed her. If she hasn't eaten, she can grab a plate anytime. I'll keep one under plastic wrap in the fridge."

"Yeah," he answered, ignoring the implication that his mom knew he'd be watching for her to return safely.

He set his favorite cowboy hat atop his head and strode into the rain, refusing to turn and give the trio behind him a look at his face. He could only imagine the expression there. His thoughts were twisted too tightly to sort, and his family was sure to read in to anything they saw.

He reminded himself that the fear he felt was unfounded. That there wasn't any reason to worry until there was. And if anyone else had missed dinner, he wouldn't have been concerned in the least. Things happened. Time slipped away. People forgot things.

The problem was, as Austin had started to say, then stopped himself, that the missing dinner guest wasn't just anyone. It was Josi. And at least half of Lincoln's thoughts about her were sure to horrify his family. They likely still saw her as the broken teen they'd rescued, but Lincoln had never known that version. When he looked at the young, blond stable manager, he saw a bright, resilient, resource-ful woman. Someone who'd survived enough of her own traumas to accept him and his. And he suspected that she, like he and his family, saw much more than she revealed.

He only hoped that none of them knew the whole ugly truth. He'd unintentionally fallen in love with her.

Cold autumn rain pelted his coat and hat as he crossed the darkened field toward his cabin, only a stone's throw from the stables. The small, matching structure beside his belonged to Josi.

A set of headlights swept down the nearby driveway, immediately making him change his direction. He wished, uselessly, for an umbrella to offer her when she emerged from her vehicle. There wasn't time to grab one from his home or the stables, but he could at least keep her company on the walk from car to cabin.

He stuffed his hands into his pockets and picked up the pace.

Josi's old SUV bounced along the well-trodden lane, then unexpectedly hooked a right. She bypassed the wide expanse of gravel where she normally parked and rolled around to the far side of a large outbuilding.

He followed, tension increasing as she shut off her lights.

A stream of rainwater spilled from the brim of his hat as he moved along the side of the building. It didn't make sense for her to park there, unless he was right, and she was in trouble. He half worried she'd drag a body from her trunk. A body he'd probably help hide if she asked.

Josi climbed clumsily from the driver's side of her SUV. She closed the door behind her. Light from her phone screen illuminated her worried face in the darkness.

Thunder rolled as Lincoln cleared his throat, using his mother's method to announce his presence and avoid alarming Josi, who'd yet to notice him. The storm effectively swallowed the sound.

His phone buzzed, and he reached for it on instinct. Josi raised her eyes to his and screamed a half step before colliding with his chest.

"Ahh!"

Lincoln's palms flipped up, the still buzzing cell phone in one hand.

She stumbled back, terror flashing in her eyes. She raised her phone, presumably to clobber him, before recognition dawned, then turned to relief. "Lincoln!" She launched at him, her cheek thumping against his chest. "Oh, thank goodness!"

He froze, arms still bent at the elbows in surrender.

"I was just calling you," she said, her body warm against his shirt, exposed by an unzipped coat. "I called the cops before I got out of the car, but I should've pulled over. I should've called sooner." Her teeth began to chatter as cold November rain poured over them.

Belatedly, his brain snapped back to his body, and his arms lowered to circle her.

She straightened abruptly, wiping her face and knocking

his hands away before he had a chance to return her embrace. "Sorry. I forgot you don't—" She motioned to him, then shook her head. "I didn't mean to—"

Lincoln grimaced. Of course, she hadn't meant to hug him. Why would she think that was reasonable when she apparently didn't think he…what? Touched people? "What's going on?" he asked, ignoring the pinch her impression of him caused in his core. Josi was clearly upset, possibly in danger. That was the important thing. "You called the police?" His voice roared against the storm, rougher and deeper than intended.

She'd also called him when she was clearly upset.

That had to count for something.

Rain swiveled paths over her flushed cheeks and darkened her long blond hair. Her gaze darted worriedly through the night. "Let's talk inside."

Lincoln dipped his chin and extended an arm in the direction of her cabin.

She headed for the stable.

A thousand worries filled his mind as he followed, then waited for her to unlock the door to her office and flip on the lights. She didn't appear injured, and her SUV had seemed undamaged. Both good signs.

"There was a gunman," she said, voice low and unsteady.

Tension seized his spine. "What do you mean, a gunman?" He pressed the door shut behind him, locking out the blowing wind and pounding rain. "Where?"

What kind of errand had she run?

Josi kicked off her sodden shoes and dropped her wet socks on top. "I mean there was a man with a gun. He took a shot at my friend, Tara. She got away, I think, but she's in danger now. I parked out of sight in case the guy somehow followed me." She cringed. "I don't think he did, but I probably shouldn't have come back here."

Lincoln tossed his hat onto an empty chair, then entered the attached half bath and snagged a stack of hand towels from the closet. He passed two to Josi, then ran another over his face and hair. He leaned against the doorjamb when he finished, soaked to the bone from his walk in the rain. "Start from the beginning."

Her blue eyes flashed to him, her body trembling, either due to the cold or excess adrenaline from the scare. Maybe both. "What if I led a deranged criminal here?" she whispered.

"Sit." He pointed to the chair at her back. She bent her knees and landed on the rolling seat.

Her bottom lip wobbled, and he kicked himself internally for a lack of finesse. This was why he made a good soldier, animal trainer and leader. He was firm and direct. It was also why he didn't do well in circumstances requiring a softer touch. "Look." He peeled himself away from the door and moved to the edge of her desk. "If the man who shot at your friend comes here, he'll leave in cuffs, or hog-tied, so that's not a scenario to worry about."

She nodded, wiping tears from her eyes and expelling a long breath. "Okay. You're right."

Fresh memories of her arms around his middle, and her soft body pressed to his, returned unbidden. He clenched his jaw, pushing aside the thoughts. He needed to concentrate. To get the full story about what happened tonight, then make a plan to protect her.

"You're mad," she said. "I knew you would be."

His brow furrowed. "I'm not mad."

"Tell your face."

Lincoln's hackles rose, and his frown deepened. He was

furious with whoever had shot at Josi and at himself for not being better at comforting her. But he was a doer. Not a talker. He thought she understood that. "What happened?" he asked again, more firmly now. "The whole story this time. Start from the beginning. I assume you called the police when you got home to alert them about the shots fired?"

"I called when I got home, because I dropped my phone on the floorboards tearing out of the motel parking lot," she corrected. "I was afraid to slow down or pull over until I got here."

His hands clenched into fists at his sides. He hated the fear in her eyes, tone and posture, and wished he could fix this. "Go on."

"I was supposed to pick up my friend, Tara, from the Bayside Motel on Route Nine. I didn't see her when I got there, so I waited a few minutes for her to come out. When she finally did, she was already running. A man with a gun followed and took a shot at her. Then he turned the gun on me. Tara ran off, and I drove away. I left her."

The tension in Lincoln's body ratcheted to the point of being in pain.

Someone had taken a shot at Josi, and there wasn't a thing he could do about it.

Slowly, she detailed her arrival at the Bayside Motel and the minutes that passed before her escape. She deflated when she finished, having apparently used the remainder of her energy. She lowered her face into waiting palms, elbows anchored on her knees. "She only sent one text. She warned me to run. Now she's not responding, and I have to find her."

"You texted her after calling the police?"

She nodded. "Then I dialed you."

Beyond the interior office window, horses shifted in

their stalls, probably wondering why they were being visited in the night. They likely sensed something was wrong.

Lincoln swiped his phone to life and thumbed through
his contacts. "I'll call Finn."

His younger brother, a Marshal's Bluff detective, was
sure to want to help. Finn and Josi were close in age. Finn
was twenty-five, just two years her senior, and the two had
been close during her first year or so with the family, a truth
that both warmed and inspired nonsensical jealousy in Lincoln. Finn was a good man and a solid friend. It was nice
that he'd been there for Josi when she'd needed someone.
Lincoln had been halfway around the world.

He raised the phone to his ear and waited.

"Put it on speaker," Josi said, straightening enough to
wrap her arms around her middle. "Please. I'd like to hear."

"Hey, man," Finn answered. "I was just going to call
you."

Lincoln pressed the speaker button. "I'm here with Josi,"
he said. "You've got us both on the line."

"Ah. Hey, Jos."

She inhaled deeply, squaring her shoulders against the
chairback. "Hey, Finn."

"I'm out here at the Bayside Motel on Route Nine. You
know why?"

Her eyes swept to Lincoln's. "Yeah. I was there tonight."

The line was eerily quiet for a long moment, save for
the muffled sound of rain.

"We got a call about a shots fired at this location," Finn
said. "A witness described an SUV similar to yours leaving
the scene. Said the driver was a woman with long blond hair."

Lincoln felt his eyes close. "Did they get a plate number on the vehicle?"

"No," Finn said.

Lincoln's eyes reopened as Josi groaned.

"The guy with the gun looked right at me," she said.

"But it's pretty dark out here and raining," Finn said. "Only one decent light in the lot."

"I parked under the light."

Lincoln's grip tightened around the cell phone, his protective instincts kicking into high gear. He threw the wadded hand towel onto the floor near Josi's shoes. "Anything else?"

"Not yet," Finn said. "But the night's young. I'll be around tomorrow to catch you up on anything I uncover. Meanwhile, I'd like to get a preliminary statement from Jos. Starting with what she was doing out here on a night like this."

As if there was ever a good reason to be at that place, Lincoln thought, passing the phone to Josi. The Bayside Motel was a haven for criminals, thugs and troublemakers.

"Hey, Linc?" Finn asked, as Josi's trembling fingers touched his.

"Yeah?"

"Do me a favor—stay with her tonight," he said. "And keep your phone close."

Lincoln looked to Josi, his thundering heart suddenly competing with the storm. He pressed one palm to the desk, anchoring himself against the thought of anyone attempting to harm her. He'd gladly do whatever it took to keep her safe, but she might not want him around for a whole night. Or another minute. It was never easy to guess what she was thinking.

He supposed he could camp out on her porch, if she wasn't comfortable having him inside.

"Lincoln can stay at my place tonight, if he wants," Josi told Finn. Her steely gaze locked with Lincoln's. "He's going to help me look for Tara in the morning."

"Good. Now tell me about Tara," Finn said.

He nodded his agreement without hesitation.

Josi set her hand over Lincoln's on the desk. The sight of her small, thin fingers against his big, scarred mitt sent heat through his core. And when she mouthed the words *thank you*, he felt a fissure form in his long-hardened heart.

Chapter Three

Josi rolled over in bed, pulling her knees to her chest, and the comforter to her chin. Her limbs were heavy and her mind clouded as she willed herself to drift back to sleep.

Memories of the previous night returned like a landslide, making her sit her upright and kicking her heart rate into a gallop. The phantom sounds of gunshots rang in her ears. Images of Tara's panicked face as she looked directly at Josi, then ran in the other direction, hit like a slap across her cheek. Josi had assumed Tara didn't see her in the darkness and rain, but by light of day, her friend's actions read differently. As if Tara had been trying to protect her. Maybe even to lead the man away, or at least not let him know Josi was there for her. She'd even sent a follow-up text. *Run*.

Tara had done what she could to protect Josi. So where was she now?

Josi pulled her phone from the nightstand to check for messages. There hadn't been anything new since she'd fallen asleep. On the couch.

Her attention jumped to the open doorway, and her galloping heart pulled into a sprint.

Lincoln had spent the night in her cabin. And he'd… carried her to bed?

Was he still there? Asleep on her couch?

She thanked her lucky stars she'd put the laundry away. If he'd seen a stack of her underthings in the basket or her bras drying on the shower rod, she might've passed away. No need to worry about the guy with a gun.

Her feet hit the floor with a thud, and her body was in motion toward the door. She paused to check her breath against one palm, then frowned and headed for the bathroom. She needed to brush her teeth and comb her hair. At least she hadn't slept in her wet clothes. The rain had forced her to change into something dry when she and Lincoln had returned from the barn. He'd stopped at his place first to grab a dry outfit, and he'd insisted she go with him. He'd barely let her out of his sight since he'd appeared behind her SUV the night before.

Josi hurried through her morning routine as quickly and quietly as possible, taking an extra moment for lip gloss and mascara. Then she hustled into the living room, trying and failing to imagine Lincoln's long, lean frame stretched out on her couch.

Surprisingly Lincoln was nowhere to be found.

A bright pink sticky note on the kitchen countertop had a message for her, written in a tight, messy scrawl. If she woke in time for breakfast, the family wanted to see her. The request was signed with a single letter. *L.* She checked the clock, then grabbed her coat. Mrs. Beaumont likely hadn't served the meal yet. Morning chores would barely be finished by now, and Mr. Beaumont oversaw those before they ate.

Josi plunged her feet into tall rubber barn boots by the door, then headed out.

The day was cool and dreary, as expected, the ground soggy from recent heavy rain. Gray clouds skated across a bleak sky. Another storm was on the way. Hopefully, this one would be strictly meteorological and not metaphorical.

She tugged the zipper on her coat and shrank into the fabric, huddling against the wind. Her small cabin sat beside Lincoln's at the far side of the stable, making it a convenient commute to work and a several-minute walk to the farmhouse.

From the quick peek she'd gotten last night, Lincoln's place was minimally decorated. Only the necessary furniture and some framed photos. She hadn't been brave enough to look too closely, unsure how long it would take him to change clothes and return for her. It hadn't been long. Her rooms were full of books, throw pillows and blankets. All the comfortable and soothing things she'd longed for as a kid and promised herself to have in abundance as an adult. Her expert thrift-shopping skills made it possible to create magazine-worthy appeal on a stable manager's budget. Another win-win where she was concerned.

They'd discussed her experience at the motel over cold sandwiches and chips from her kitchen, hypothesizing reasons for Tara to have been there and who the man might be. Eventually, Josi had turned on the television and navigated to the local news, hoping to catch any revelations about the case. The shooting hadn't even been mentioned, and she'd apparently fallen asleep. Leaving Lincoln alone.

Based on the stacks of her favorite romantic suspense novels dotting every flat surface from desk to windowsill, her deep fascination with cowboys was no longer a secret.

She cringed.

At least he didn't know he'd been the one to kick-start that particular fantasy.

She pressed thoughts of him from her mind with a purposeful thrust, then focused on the upcoming meal instead. She was sure Mrs. Beaumont and at least one of Lincoln's brothers had caught her staring at Lincoln in the past. They'd never said anything, but they'd definitely seen. Now that she'd spent so much time with him outside of work, even for this awful reason, she felt uncomfortably exposed. And her crush felt more like an ugly bruise.

She wet her lips, and the taste of cherry-flavored gloss nearly caused her to misstep. She rarely wore makeup and never to work. Every Beaumont at the table would notice. Some might even guess the reason. Though, probably not Lincoln, who was endlessly oblivious to her attempts at flirtation. She pulled a tissue from the pocket of her coat and wiped the shine from her lips. There wasn't anything to be done about the mascara.

Her pace slowed as another thought came to mind. If the whole family knew Lincoln had stayed at her place all night, would they have questions? Concerns?

Probably not, she realized. Josi was a full five years younger than Lincoln, and the Beaumonts still looked at her as if she was a teen in need of protecting. They'd never suspect anything inappropriate could happen between her and Lincoln. In fact, she thought ironically, her dreams that Lincoln would one day realize he was madly in love with her were probably evidence to support the fact she was still the kid everyone saw her as.

She sighed and shored up her nerves with each determined, if somewhat reluctant, step. Everyone would want to know she was okay and hear the story of the motel and gunman from her lips. They'd want to comfort and reassure her, because they were wonderful people. And that was where her thoughts should be. With Tara, wherever she was. Not on Lincoln.

The farmhouse's front door opened as she reached the

steps, and Lincoln moved onto the porch. The tiny smile she loved played at the corners of his mouth, but he quickly tamped it down.

"Waiting for me?" she teased.

He dipped his chin once, eyes narrowing. "Yeah." He shoved his hands into his pockets, the exposed skin beneath his short sleeves pebbling from the frigid wind. "I didn't want to leave you this morning, but I thought you might prefer to get ready without me hanging around. I've kept an eye on your place and the lane."

"Thanks."

The door behind him sucked open, jostling a grapevine wreath covered in faux autumn leaves and tiny pumpkins. Mrs. Beaumont hustled out. "Oh, you two! It's freezing!" She tugged her son backward and extended her free arm toward Josi. "Come inside!"

Lincoln watched as Josi allowed his mother to sweep her into the home.

She felt his eyes on her all the way to the kitchen.

"There she is," Mr. Beaumont said, greeting her with a warm hug. "How are you doing this morning? Were you able to get a little rest last night? We heard all about what happened. I expect these guys to get into harm's way from time to time, but we try to keep you safe." He motioned to Lincoln's brothers, Finn, Austin and Dean, already seated at the table. One detective and two private investigators.

Josi took one of the empty chairs, and Mr. Beaumont sat across from her.

Mrs. Beaumont and Lincoln followed, each carrying a tray of food from the counter. They placed the items at the table's center with others already in wait.

"Coffee?" Finn asked, passing a carafe in her direction.

"Thanks." She accepted the vessel and smiled at her

family. Whatever else happened, she was thankful for this group.

Mrs. Beaumont lowered herself gracefully onto the chair beside her husband, and Lincoln took the seat next to Josi.

Josi fixed her attention on Finn. "How'd it go last night at the motel? Any leads on Tara?"

He shook his head. "Not yet."

"Any signs she was hit when that guy fired at her?" Josi had worried herself sick over the possibility Tara might've taken a bullet before sending that final text warning Josi to run.

"No traces of blood, but the rains were pretty heavy last night," Finn said. "My men are working the crime scene more thoroughly this morning. With a little luck, the wind didn't blow those shell casings too far. Ballistics will try to match them to the gun or another crime in the database. We can find the owner from there."

Platters of food made their ways around the table, passed hand to hand, as Finn spoke. Muffins and breads. Fresh fruits and yogurt. Jellies and jams. A lidded casserole with quiche. Another with sliced bacon and sausage links.

Josi selected toast and jam, fruit and eggs, then nabbed a slice of bacon. She filled the mug before her with coffee from the carafe and sipped gingerly as she sent up more prayers for Tara's safety.

What on earth had she gotten mixed up in that would cause someone to shoot at her? The Tara that Josi knew was quiet and a little shy. Smart and determined. Nothing that suggested she'd be in a room at a shady motel with a gunman.

Mrs. Beaumont watched Josi closely as she ate. The expression was maternal, as always, but with an edge of curiosity Josi hadn't seen before. "We were glad to hear you accepted Lincoln's offer to stay with you last night."

Josi stilled, unsure how to respond. "Finn suggested it was a good idea."

"Everyone agrees," Mrs. Beaumont said sweetly.

Josi glanced to Finn, then Lincoln. The former appeared amused. The latter, furious.

"We know how independent you are," their mom continued. "It probably felt like having a babysitter, but it wasn't intended that way."

Josi cringed at her word choice and turned her focus to her meal. If she kept her mouth full, no one would expect her to respond.

Finn forked a bite of quiche, then he set down his fork while he chewed. "Jos, you said you hadn't spoken to Tara in a long while before last night, but do you have any idea what she might've been up to?"

"None." Josi bit her lip, the faint taste of cherry still clinging there. "We haven't spoken much since her brother died." Maybe the grief had sent her into a spiral. "She apologized for calling me to ask a favor, which was odd, because we really were close once. She said she wasn't sure who else she could trust."

Finn leaned forward, eyebrows up. "Were those her words?"

Josi paused, reaching mentally backward for the conversation and for Tara's exact statement. "I think so. Why?"

Dean kicked back in his chair, coffee mug cradled between his palms. "Big difference between deciding who she could ask and who she could trust. Deciding who to ask might mean she wasn't sure who'd help if she needed it, or even who'd be available."

"You've got to know someone a little to ask for a favor," Austin added, running with his brother's train of thought. "You've got to know them well to trust them."

Lincoln shifted at her side, his arm brushing hers as he moved. "It goes deeper than that," Lincoln said. "If I had something I didn't want everyone to know, I could ask anyone at this table to keep my secret. They're all family. I know them all well. But I wouldn't necessarily trust any of them to keep some things to themselves."

Austin pointed his fork at Lincoln and winked, then returned to his breakfast with a hearty laugh.

Everyone else became suddenly, and equally, amused.

Josi frowned, missing the humor in the topic. "I guess if Tara had a secret she didn't want getting out, I'd be a good choice for her call. I don't know anyone in her current circle, or if she has one. And I have no connection to our old friends, if she's even still running with any of them."

Finn nodded, sobering from the joke Josi had clearly missed. "Do you know if she lost the house she was renting?"

The idea of Tara without a home soured Josi's stomach. "What do you mean?" The fear of having nowhere to live was a burden Josi had carried for many years. Especially as she'd gotten older and fewer foster families were open to taking in teens. Thankfully, Tara's older brother had returned from the marines when she'd needed him most, and he'd taken her in before she landed on the streets. Just the way the Beaumonts had brought Josi to the ranch.

"According to the desk clerk at the motel," Finn said, "Tara had been staying in that room for a couple of weeks and paying cash."

So she hadn't gone there on a whim, and not to party or hook up.

She'd been living there.

Josi felt her features bunch and her nose wrinkle. "I thought she still lived downtown, on Bay View."

Finn lifted his chin. "That's the street listed on her driver's license. I'm headed over there on my way to the station. We should probably talk about your SUV before I go."

Josi pulled the key from her pocket. "I can move it if it's in the way. I was freaked out last night and didn't want to leave it in the open."

"That was smart," Finn said. "Dad and Dean cleared out some space inside the storage building this morning. Leave the key and I'll move it in there when I leave. Just due diligence," he added. "Until we figure out who had the gun and why."

"But Lincoln said he'd help me look for Tara this morning."

Mrs. Beaumont waved a carefree hand in her direction. "Linc can drive you anywhere you need to go. And if you're with him, we won't worry so much."

Josi's lips parted but words failed to come. She'd assumed she'd do the driving, and he'd come along in case of trouble. Making him her personal chauffer was a lot more than he'd agreed to.

Lincoln wiped his mouth on a napkin, then set the cloth on the table. "I figured we'd visit Tara's work. Make a circle around town, ask a few questions. Someone has to know something that will point us in her direction."

The family all nodded, apparently in agreement with his plan.

Josi's heart swelled. Lincoln wasn't just going with her as muscle in case of trouble. He was actively partnering with her on the project.

As if she needed one more reason to be a goner for this man.

Chapter Four

By three o'clock, Lincoln had finished his work at the stable. The riding lessons were over for the day, and Josi was in her office wrapping up things on her end as well. They'd soon shower, change and begin their reconnaissance mission to garner information on Josi's missing friend. With some luck, the outing would involve the woman's safe recovery as well.

He and Josi had never left the ranch together, and it would be nice if everything went smoothly, and maybe he got to be a hero. Unfortunately, the only type of luck Lincoln seemed to have lately was bad.

Nerves coiled and tensed in his limbs as he approached the open office door, making his footfalls as loud as possible. No one liked being startled, and Josi was already, understandably, on edge.

Her eyes met his instantly, and were a little wider than usual. "I was just finishing up." She powered off her computer and grabbed her jacket from a hook near the door. "Ready?"

He nodded, watching her carefully as she moved. Coordinating his life with someone else's hadn't been a necessity in a very long time. Even growing up with siblings and the years spent in the military hadn't prepared him for this. "Should we shower first?"

Josi stopped abruptly. "What do you mean?"

"I can grab my things and take them to your cabin, or you're welcome to wait while I get cleaned up." Lincoln shifted his weight and gripped the back of his neck. "Either way, I'd like to stick together, if you don't mind."

Her cheeks flushed, and the misunderstanding became apparent.

He fought the knee-jerk urge to react. *No growling. No cussing. Or anything else that might make matters worse*, he warned himself internally. "I can wait on your porch during your shower."

Josi nodded slowly, as if struggling to come back from wherever her thoughts had taken her. Hopefully not to a place that labeled him as deeply inappropriate, or worse, a pervert. "If I promise to hurry, can we split up instead? Shower and meet back here in twenty minutes?" she suggested, averting her big blue eyes.

He considered the possibility. Hated it. But he had no solid reason to protest, and he didn't want to start their time together off-site with unnecessary tension. No need to paint himself as more of a pain in her backside than she surely already thought he was. He dipped his chin in reluctant agreement, then they made their way home to neighboring cabins.

Lincoln took a seat on her porch fourteen minutes later, freshly showered and hat in hand. The idea of being Josi's personal protector had been on his mind almost as much as the woman herself. He was responsible for her safety, which meant he had a reason to spend as much time with her as she'd allow, and no one would question it. He could ask all the questions he had bottled up without seeming nosy. He'd just be passing time. Getting to know her. Putting her at ease.

His family knew far more about Josi than he did. They loved and respected her. They'd brought her into the fold long before he'd come home.

He had catching up to do.

The door to her cabin opened, and Josi stepped out, dressed in nice-fitting jeans, sneakers and a black wool coat that hugged her narrow hips and waist. Her signature scent hit him with the wind. Coconuts and vanilla. No matter the season or weather, Josi smelled like a lazy summer day at the beach.

"Oh." She stopped short, pressing a hand to her chest. "You're here. I thought I'd beat you."

"I just got here."

She bit her lower lip, probably deciding if he was telling the truth.

Lincoln stood and pulled keys from his pocket, and she moved to his side without another word.

He could vividly remember the moment he'd met her, in the days following his return from the military. She'd talked to him when he didn't talk back. Sang while she worked. Generally made no show of being uncomfortable around a near stranger who was still half-haunted by his experiences a world away. She'd brought books to his cabin in the evenings. Bottled water and snacks during the day. She'd left both on the steps, where he would find them, but never knocked or intruded on his need for space. When he was finally ready to work, she behaved as if it was any other day.

For all those things and more, Lincoln owed her far more than a temporary position as a bodyguard. He owed her his life. There wasn't any way to know what might've happened to him if not for her presence in those early, dark days following his discharge. But he was certain he wouldn't be the man he was now without her.

Josi stole glances at him as they crossed the field, then climbed into his truck.

He started the engine and adjusted the heater. Temperatures were falling fast in their small coastal town and would likely continue to decline for the next few days, until all the storms had passed.

The radio powered on with the truck, delivering the tail end of a popular country song, and Lincoln shifted into gear while Josi buckled up.

They made it as far as the road at the end of the driveway before the station's DJ returned with news of the previous night's shooting.

Lincoln turned up the volume as he navigated the pickup onto the smooth dark ribbon of asphalt leading away from home.

"Two women were reported as targets. Security-camera footage confirms one woman escaped on foot, the other in her SUV, both were believed to be local, and the lucky driver? Josi Roberts, a stable manager at the Beaumont Ranch, a long-established haven in our community."

Josi made a small choking sound that spiked Lincoln's growing irritation.

He tapped his dashboard screen, teeth gritted as he commanded, "Call Finn."

"I know," his brother said, without greeting and before a single ring came through the speakers. "We're working to get her name removed from the story, but it's already been posted to the station's web page. Before you lose your patience with me, please remember we all love Josi, and she has you. Tara's on her own. We've got to stay focused on finding her."

Lincoln's traitorous gaze flickered sideways, seeking Josi, then he returned his eyes to the road. Had she understood the implication in his brother's words? They all loved her. Including Lincoln. Would she assume he loved her the way they did? Like a sister?

"What's wrong?" Her voice drew his gaze once more. Her bright eyes were slightly narrowed, her pretty lips in a frown. "You look affronted."

"He always looks affronted," Finn said. "I'll do what I can to fix this," he promised.

"I know," she said, dragging her attention to the screen. "We trust you, and like you said, I'm safe with Lincoln. Any leads on Tara?"

Pleasure swept through him at her words. He resisted the urge to smile. Josi's name had been leaked to the media, then announced on the local radio station and posted online, so he would smile after he knew she was truly safe.

"Nothing yet," Finn said.

Josi crossed her legs, then quickly uncrossed them. "It's been nearly twenty-four hours. She hasn't responded to my texts, and my calls go straight to voice mail. What does that mean? Is the phone dead? Is it off?"

"I'm working with Tech to track the device," he said. "If the phone's still on, we'll be able to narrow the search. I've got an incoming call now. Keep an eye on my brother, would ya?"

"Keep me in the loop," she said, ignoring Finn's goofy request.

The call disconnected, and Josi huffed lightly. "We should probably start with the home Tara shared with her brother. At dinner, Finn made it sound as if her address hasn't changed."

"On Bay View?" Lincoln asked, recalling the conversation clearly.

"Yeah. A yellow cottage near the cul-de-sac. I don't remember the address, but I'll know the house when I see it."

Lincoln took the next left, heading toward downtown.

"If she's not there, we can try her work, or reach out to the old friend group Tara and I shared. She might still be in touch with some of them."

"Sounds good." Both his grip and his jaw tightened. Now that her name had been leaked, his time with her felt significantly less fun, and more high-stakes.

The thin silver lining, he supposed, was that she was with him, and he was better trained, more capable and more highly motivated to protect her than anyone.

JOSI WATCHED THE familiar surroundings fly past her window as Lincoln piloted his massive truck into town. The interior smelled of fresh air, sunshine and hay. There were also hints of the spearmint gum he often chewed mixed with the aftershave he sometimes wore. His clothes and boots were well-worn and obviously old. As far as she could tell, he hadn't spent money on much of anything since his return from the military, except his truck. The behemoth was everything a cowboy could want. Big and shiny, formidable and expensive, but not just for show. The vehicle worked as hard as its owner, hauling, towing and transporting everything from hay bales to horse trailers on an almost daily basis. His priorities were clearly based on activities, and not appearances. One more thing she appreciated. Hard work rarely steered a person wrong.

She'd often wondered if Lincoln spent so many hours in motion to keep his mind busy. Perhaps to avoid the thoughts he wished he never had. That had been her reasoning once. These days, however, she spent extra time at work because he was there.

Now she was inside his truck. And they were alone in the smallest space they'd ever shared. If only the reason for their being in this position was anything other than the search for a missing friend.

A beaded chain and black dog tag swung from the rear-view mirror. She'd learned, after a quick internet search during Lincoln's early days home, that the color signified his position as a US Army Ranger. He'd barely spoken then, and she'd had innumerable questions.

The truck slowed, and her thoughts returned to the moment, eyes searching the row of older homes on each side of the road. Tara's neighborhood was blue-collar and filled with young families. Children rode bikes on sidewalks and played in the streets. No adults in sight. She supposed most of the parents in this area worked outside the home and would return after five. Meanwhile, the kids were likely fresh off the school bus and releasing seven hours of pent-up energy.

"There." She spotted the familiar yellow cottage and pointed. The home was in need of fresh paint and a little yard work, but it was nicer than a lot of the places she and Tara had lived as youths. "Grass is long."

"Finn said Tara was staying at the motel lately," Lincoln said.

He stopped at the end of the driveway, surveying the scene. No cars. No garage. No indication anyone was home. He parked at the curb and settled the engine. His keen gaze traveled over the homes, lawns and playing children.

"I'm going to knock," she said, opening her door to climb out.

In a perfect scenario, Tara would invite them in and explain what was going on. Then Josi and the Beaumonts could protect her while Finn located and arrested the gunman.

Lincoln followed her silently, his looming presence sending chills over her skin.

Whatever came at her today, Josi would be safe. It was unlikely anyone in Marshal's Bluff could get the best of Lincoln, and she had a feeling he'd protect her at all costs. He was all about completing assignments.

She knocked on Tara's door and waited, then rang the bell when no one answered. A few seconds later, she peeked through the front window. A small split between drawn curtains provided a glimpse of the tidy living room.

"What do you see?" Lincoln asked, stepping closer to her side.

She cupped her hands against the sides of her face to block the sun and help her focus. "Couch. Books on the coffee table. Framed photos on the fireplace. Looks like her stuff."

"Signs of a struggle?"

She shook her head. "Nope."

"Signs of a pet?"

Josi straightened, heart suddenly in her throat. "I don't think so." She hadn't thought of that possibility. She set a hand on his coat sleeve, moved by his concern for an animal that Tara may have had.

His gaze locked with hers for a long beat before dropping to her fingers.

She pulled back, tucking her hand into her pocket. Lincoln barely spoke. He probably wasn't big on touch either. So why couldn't she seem to stop touching him? "Tara wasn't the nurturing type," she said, redirecting his attention. "She swore she'd never have kids. Her childhood was rough. Marcus took care of her. Surviving was the real goal. She never wanted any added strings or responsibilities."

He nodded, then swept an arm outward, motioning her back toward the truck. "What about you?"

She frowned as they parted ways at the curb, him to the driver's side and her to the passenger door.

"How do you feel about strings?" he asked.

"Pets or kids?"

He lifted and dropped one shoulder before climbing behind the wheel.

She hurried to slide inside and catch his eye once more. "I love animals, and I get to hang out with the livestock every day at the ranch. It's like having a couple dozen various pets. I'd like kids too, I think, someday, but I didn't exactly have a decent role model, so—"

"You don't want to mess them up," he said.

"Yeah." Her heart fell at his words. He understood. Was it because he had a similar idea about her?

"I think the same thing about myself."

Her jaw dropped. "What do you mean? You have the perfect parental examples."

He started the engine and turned the wheel. "But I'm not the same kid they raised. Parts of me are broken that won't ever be the same."

"But they will heal," she said, suddenly sticking up for him, despite the fact he was his own attacker. "Broken bones are strongest at the points where they healed."

Lincoln lanced her with sharp green eyes, stealing her words and breath.

A round of riotous laughter drew their attention to the cul-de-sac, where a pair of boys bounced basketballs in a driveway.

He rolled slowly toward the kids and powered down his window. "Hey."

The kids advanced on the truck, lips parted in what looked like awe.

"You know the lady who lives there?" Lincoln asked, pointing to the yellow cottage.

They nodded, eyes wide as they took in the big black truck and its driver.

"Seen her lately?" Lincoln asked, voice low and thick with authority.

They shook their heads.

Josi guessed the kids to be in middle school, maybe sixth or seventh grade. Both wore ribbed white tank tops and basketball shorts. She leaned in Lincoln's direction, projecting her voice through the open window. "Does she have a dog or cat?"

"No, ma'am," the taller kid said. "It's just Ms. Tara."

Lincoln looked over his shoulder at Josi, eyes narrowed. "They talk now? All they did was move their heads for me."

She grinned, and his lips pulled into a frown.

Josi waved to the kids. "Thank you. If you see her, will you let her know her friend came to see her?"

"Yes, ma'am."

Lincoln stepped on the gas pedal and the truck rolled away before Josi could tell the kids her name. In hindsight, maybe that was best.

They left the neighborhood more quickly than they'd entered, making unnecessary turns and breaking the residential speed limit.

"Are we in a hurry?" she asked, bracing a palm against the dashboard as Lincoln took another speedy right.

Lincoln grunted. "I think we were being followed, but I lost him." He glanced at her, then back to his rearview mirror. "I haven't seen them in a couple of blocks. I'm just putting space between us now."

"We were being followed?" Josi's heart rate hiked. "Since when?"

"Since we pulled away from the curb outside her door. I noticed while we spoke to those kids."

Josi checked her sideview mirror, then angled in her seat for a better look at the empty road behind them. She hadn't seen anything unusual, other than the change in Lincoln's driving. Her stomach knotted with memories of the night before. Of a man with a gun, willing to take a shot at the back of a terrified woman already running away.

"What's next?" Lincoln asked, falling into the steady pulse of downtown traffic.

All around them, storefronts and sidewalks had been adorned with festive fall and holiday decor. Hay bales and cornstalks. Silk autumn-colored leaves and twinkle lights. Even a few early Christmas trees glowed beyond glass windows.

"Pawnshop, I think." Most people spent more time with coworkers than their families. Hopefully, Tara's coworkers would know more about where she was or what she'd been up to recently than her young neighbors. "She worked there last year. If she moved on, maybe someone will know where she works now."

Lincoln initiated his turn signal and changed lanes. "That's not in a great area of town."

"Nope." Josi gave Lincoln a fresh once-over, seeing him through a new lens. "You're going to stand out down there. Folks might even think you're a cop."

He snorted. "I look like a cop?"

"Maybe not, but you definitely look like trouble."

Mischief flashed in his eyes and his lips curved into a slow, sexy grin. "What am I supposed to do about that?"

Josi's mouth opened before she thought better of it. "I

guess we need a reasonable explanation for why someone who clearly doesn't belong is in the area. Since you'll be with me, you should probably pretend to be my boyfriend."

Chapter Five

Josi's body tensed as they traveled the roads of her past, through intersections where the ghosts of street fights still sent shivers over her skin. Born to a mom with no business raising a daughter and without the good sense to give her baby to people who could protect her, Josi had lived a hundred equally awful lives before she'd been old enough to drive. Like most of her friends and foster siblings, she'd been in a dozen houses before middle school. Pulled from her mother's negligent care for temporary, emergency placement, only to be returned to her home a few days, weeks or months later. No roots. No security. Nothing of her own. Unless she counted the emotional pain, scars, neglect and trauma. All permanent gifts from her mother.

"You okay?" Lincoln asked, his voice jarring her from the dreary trip down memory lane.

"Yeah."

He probably heard the lie. Her answer had been too thin and breathy. But he didn't comment. A few blocks later, they parked outside Petey's Pawnshop.

Red block letters on the glass encouraged folks to come inside. *Get a deal! Trade stuff for cash!*

Walking the stretch of sidewalk to the door brought another wave of unwanted memories. Underage drinking. The scent of marijuana. Friends hocking things they'd stolen for money to buy more pot or beer. Petey always cut a deal, pretending he didn't know how a group of teens like them had gotten their hands on designer bags and jewelry. When Tara had come to him for employment at eighteen, he'd given her a job. Josi supposed she could thank him for that.

She was still unclear where Petey stood in the division between good and evil. Or where anyone stood for that matter.

She smoothed sweat-slicked palms against her hips and took a centering breath as Lincoln opened and held the door for her. Her ears rang and heart pounded as they stepped into the display room of miscellaneous items. Sad aisles filled with stuff people were forced to let go. Things traded for drug money, bill money, bail money, or maybe a second chance.

Things a bunch of unsupervised, lawless kids had pinched for fun.

Lincoln matched her pace, walking so closely that his arm brushed hers. Then the gentle pressure of his hand against her back caused her steps to stutter. His cool green eyes were watching when she jerked her gaze to his. "Would you prefer to hold hands?"

Josi's mouth opened, and a small unintelligible sound emerged.

Lincoln raised one eyebrow by a tiny fraction. "Don't your boyfriends usually hold your hand?"

She nodded, slammed back to the present by her earlier suggestion. She'd assumed he wasn't on board when he'd failed to respond. Then she'd promptly died of humiliation, only to be resurrected by the changing scenery outside her window and thoughts of something worse. Her life before the Beaumonts.

Lincoln's large, calloused palm pressed against her hand, and she inhaled a shaky breath. He studied her face as he spread her fingers and slid his in between.

A thrill coursed through her as they began to walk once more.

"Well, looky here," a deep baritone boomed from the distance a moment before Petey appeared, wiping his hands on a shop rag.

If Josi had to guess, he'd probably been watching them via security cameras since they'd entered, maybe before, if the cameras out front were working.

Tattoos stretched from the short sleeves of Petey's navy T-shirt to his wrists. Similar patterns of ink climbed his neck from collar to chin. His hair was grayer than she remembered. More lines and creases had gathered on his face. He was still big. Tall and broad, but not as intimidating as she'd once imagined.

A pair of younger men in flannel shirts and jeans emerged a moment later, from the densely packed aisles.

"Petey," Josi said. "Any chance you've seen Tara today?"

"No," He shook his head. "Y'all seen Tara?" he asked, tossing her question to the others.

The younger duo smiled, shaking their heads. One dragged a hand through unkempt hair. The other scratched his bearded chin. Nothing about their expressions was friendly.

The blond man narrowed his eyes. "What do you want with Tara?"

Petey clucked his tongue. "They're friends, Dustin," he said. "Like sisters once. Doesn't she tell you anything?"

Dustin's cheeks darkened as his eyes flashed back to Josi, then climbed Lincoln from head to toe in careful evaluation. "How come I never seen you with her?"

Lincoln squeezed her hand. "She's been with me."

The air left the room as all three men stared.

Lincoln straightened slowly to his full height, and the energy around them became erratic. Something in his low tenor voice was new to Josi and, honestly, a little frightening.

"Who the hell are you?" Dustin asked.

Lincoln stared, clearly unmotivated to answer, and possibly considering how best to knock him out for swearing at him.

"He's my boyfriend," Josi answered. "I am Tara's friend. We were supposed to hang out, but I can't reach her."

Dustin didn't look convinced. "When were you going to hang out?"

Josi wiggled free from Lincoln and pulled her phone from her bag, then retrieved her call log. She scrolled to the point where Tara called her, then all the times she'd tried calling her back. "She called. We made plans. Then she just went silent."

Dustin's gaze jumped to Petey.

"You're not the only one asking those questions," Petey said. He bent forward at the waist, resting meaty forearms on the glass countertop between them. "Someone was already in here looking for her."

"Who?" Lincoln asked.

"Cops?" Josi guessed.

Petey sucked his teeth. "Nah, but they called a bit ago. They're coming this afternoon."

Lincoln's hand skimmed across her back, fingers tightening at her waist as he pulled her to his side. "Is Tara in some kind of trouble?"

The younger duo exchanged quiet words then headed for the door. They didn't stop until they were outside.

"Dustin worries about her," Petey said. "But she'll turn up. Tara—" He chuckled, expression softening slightly.

"She's tough, and she doesn't have time for boys or non-sense." He gave Josi a closer look. "You used to be the same way. Seems like a lot's changed. You've grown up nice."

Something like a growl rumbled in Lincoln's chest, and Petey straightened.

Taller than most people at close to six foot four, he was at least twenty years older than Lincoln and a hundred pounds heavier. If his plan was to intimidate, it was his unlucky day.

She stepped in front of her new boyfriend, still a little turned on by that growl and forced a tight smile for Petey. "If you see Tara, let her know I'm looking for her. If she's in some kind of trouble, I can help."

Josi turned and tugged Lincoln's arm, urging him to follow.

He stood his ground, eyes fixed on Petey far longer than was comfortable for anyone, before relenting to her silent request.

When they reached the sidewalk, a familiar voice rose from around the corner. It seemed Dustin and his friend hadn't gone far.

"She'll probably show up at Brady's tonight," one voice said. "Don't sweat it. Tara never misses a party."

Lincoln unlocked the truck and opened Josi's door. He waited while she climbed inside before rounding the hood to join her. He hadn't helped her into his ride when they'd left the farm or Tara's house. Apparently this was the Lincoln Beaumont girlfriend experience.

Add in the way he hadn't stopped touching her while they were in the pawnshop, and the protective growl…Josi would likely never recover.

LINCOLN PULLED INTO TRAFFIC, mind bucking. He hated the way the beefy pawnshop guy had ogled Josi. The two skinny punks hadn't been much better, but the older man seemed to think he had some kind of claim over her because he'd known her when she was a kid. Not only was the age difference unacceptable, and the way he looked at her completely disrespectful, but that guy also didn't know anything about Josi Roberts. Whoever she'd been when she'd last walked into that shop, it wasn't the same woman seated beside him today.

He reached across the seat between them and set a hand on her knee—he felt protective, proud and...*out of line*. His eyes slid closed a moment, then reopened to focus on the road. They were pretending to be romantically involved for the sake of finding Tara, but that pretense should've stopped when they were away from questioning eyes.

The role had just been so easy to fall into. Comfortable, natural and nice.

Now, his hand was on her knee, and it did not belong there. He locked his jaw and raised his arm, reaching quickly for the radio instead.

Josi caught his hand and settled it back on her knee. She curled small fingers around his palm and squeezed. As if touching him was the most normal thing in the world.

A barrage of hopeful thoughts took shape in his mind, and he fought the smile trying to form.

The flash of black in his rearview mirror put an instant stop to the high. The car from Tara's neighborhood was back, and it was gaining speed behind them.

Instinct kicked his muscles into gear, and he pressed the gas pedal to the floor.

Josi yelped softly beside him, releasing his hand when he pulled it back to the steering wheel. "Same car from before?" she asked, angling for a look behind them.

"Looks like it."

Lincoln powered into the next turn, and the truck fish-tailed around the corner. His vehicle easily recovered and launched forward once more, gaining speed and distance while the driver behind them struggled for control. Lincoln would've snorted at the complete ineptitude had his heart rate not kicked into an unbidden sprint, dividing his focus. He hadn't had a panic attack in months, but he recognized the signs. He intentionally kept his routines as predictable as possible, and that kept the attacks under control. Except now, he was unexpectedly calling on the offensive driving experience he'd picked up in another place and time, and his mind was filling with unwanted images of destruction.

A fervent curse slipped through his gritted teeth.

The cars and pedestrians around them became little more than blurs. His vision tunneled, and the upcoming traffic light turned yellow. Lincoln stomped on the gas, earning a series of honks as his truck sailed through the intersection and careened away.

His breaths grew shorter and more shallow as he pushed aside the intruding thoughts and focused on the moment at hand. Then his limbs began to tremble.

"Pull behind the school," Josi said softly. "No one's there."

He followed her instructions, veering into the turn lane, then onto the road surrounding Marshal Bluff High School's expansive campus. They rocked to a stop outside an auxiliary gym.

His eyelids closed, and his chest tightened. His hands fumbled to release his seat belt. He wanted out. Wanted air. Wanted to be anywhere Josi wouldn't see him lose control, but it was already too late.

Sounds of chopper blades and gunfire echoed in his mind. Images of his team crossing enemy lines on a recovery mission gone wrong. The realization they'd been spotted.

"Lincoln," Josi demanded. "Nod if you can hear me."

He sucked in a ragged breath that raked like claws down his windpipe. He wasn't in the desert anymore. He was home. He was with Josi. And she needed him to protect her.

"Lincoln," she repeated. "Nod."

A small clicking sound turned his head in her direction. Not a gun clip inserted. Not a hammer pulled.

She'd released her safety belt and turned on the seat to face him. Then, slowly, she moved in his direction, big blue eyes glued to his. "You see me?"

He lowered his chin in acknowledgment.

"And you hear me."

This time, he managed a nod.

"You know me?"

Adrenaline raced through his veins, gonging in his ears and causing his teeth to chatter.

"May I touch you?" she asked, voice lower and less demanding.

He cringed, hating that she had to see him like this. That he had to be like this. And that even years later, some part of him was still being tortured in another land.

Josi's small hands found his, and suddenly everything else fell away. His senses heightened, and he was hyperfocused on that single point of connection. She stroked his aching hands and peeled his fingers from the steering wheel.

"Lincoln," she whispered, softer still. "You are safe, and so am I. We are unharmed, and we aren't in any danger now."

He met her normally doe-eyed gaze, and found something fierce in her stare.

Josi raised his palm to her heart and pressed it against her breastbone.

She'd unfastened her coat to allow him access, and she moved her free hand to his chest. "Feel that? That's my heart beating fast and strong. I feel yours too. We're together, and we're okay. Count the beats. One, two, three, four…"

The cadence of her voice and the rhythm of her heart slowly carried him back to her.

"You feel my touch," she said. "You hear my voice. Can you see anything blue nearby?"

His gaze snapped back to hers. The fire he'd seen there earlier was gone, replaced with something else entirely. Not fear or pity, as he'd expected. Not even kindness or compassion. Something more like…understanding.

"Sky."

"Right." She smiled, and he did too. Because Josi saw him. Really saw him. And she wasn't afraid or upset by what she found.

"Anything red?"

"Gym sign."

"Good." She smiled. "Feeling better?"

The tension in his muscles eased and he removed his hand from her chest. "How'd you know what to do?"

She eased away by a fraction. "I had panic attacks for most of my life. Even after I came to the ranch," she said. "The animals helped me recenter when I felt myself spinning out. Before that, a friend talked me through them."

"Tara?" he asked, guessing.

"No, but she's helped me through a lot. Tara's tough in all the ways I will never be. Her brother made sure she could protect and handle herself. They both shared as much as they could of that with me."

Lincoln's rattled mind hated every possible reason Josi

had for suffering as he did. She was too good and kind to have ever been anything other than loved and cherished. "I'm sorry."

She scooted back to her seat, a sad smile on her lips. "I don't know if you're apologizing for your attack or mine, but don't. We're survivors. I'd rather deal with episodes like this for the rest of my life, thankful that I lived, rather than the alternative."

His mouth opened and, as usual, words failed.

She buckled up and turned her head to face him. "I know how the people at the pawnshop must look to you. I feel ashamed of how they look to me now. Guarded. Hard. Mean. But I spent a lifetime in that world, before yours. I was just like them not long ago, but I received opportunities they didn't. And each time I learn to do better, I try. A lot of folks don't know. Some are just stuck. I like to think everyone is out here doing their best."

Lincoln turned the truck back to the road and headed for home. "I don't care about the people at the pawnshop," he said. "And I don't know what you think I see when I look at them or you, but you're probably wrong on both counts."

"They're good people," she said, apparently still determined to make some kind of point. "It can be hard, not knowing who to trust."

"Are we still talking about the crew at the pawnshop?"

Josi turned away and dropped her hands into her lap. "I didn't know the younger guys we saw, and I only knew Petey secondhand through friends. But I know all about the parties Dustin and the other guy mentioned. Brady's bonfires are legendary."

Lincoln rolled his shoulders and stretched his neck, tipping his head from side to side. Thankful the attack had passed. He had to get ahold of himself if he was going to play bodyguard to Josi. He couldn't afford another attack. Not with a gunman on the hunt and a black sedan out there looking to give chase.

His truck picked up speed along the scenic byway.

A large setting sun painted distant waves in shades of crimson to gold, lighting the ocean on fire.

"We should eat dinner early," Josi said, pulling his attention back to her.

"Hungry?" He glanced at the clock. It was nearing dinner, he supposed. The afternoon had flown.

"Always," she said. "Plus, tonight we have a bonfire to attend."

Chapter Six

Lincoln paced the gravel outside his truck after dinner, his focus bouncing between the distant road and Josi's cabin. She was getting ready for the bonfire, where she hoped to get answers about Tara. He was sorting his thoughts. Logically, he knew he'd shaken their tail before pulling into the high-school parking lot. Whoever had followed them from Tara's home to the pawnshop had been caught at the traffic light he'd run, but that didn't mean he and Josi couldn't be found on the ranch. The local radio station had given her name and place of employment. Even if the criminals in question had somehow missed the broadcast, Lincoln, unlike his brothers, hadn't bothered to conceal his name when purchasing his truck. His job as a ranch hand generally kept him out of danger. He'd had no reason to hide and no one was looking for him...until a few hours ago. Now enough time had passed for someone with connections to run his license-plate number, get his name and his address. Lincoln's only measure of hope was that whoever had taken those shots outside the Bayside Motel was more of a civil menace than a criminal mastermind.

Then again, even the most unintelligent of thugs worked for someone.

Movement in his peripheral vision pulled his gaze from

the road to a petite and curvy figure headed his way. Josi had traded her wool peacoat and sneakers for a black leather motorcycle jacket and matching boots. Her hair was down and she'd put on more makeup than he'd ever seen her wear. Dark lashes and liner accentuated her big blue eyes. Stain the color of strawberries highlighted her cheeks and lips. She'd transformed from the literal girl next door to a vixen in the space of an hour, and the contrast caused his brain to misfire.

Worse, he had to escort her to a party looking this way. Protecting the sweet stable manager was one job. Playing bodyguard to the woman approaching him felt like a whole other level of duty, and some mixture of the soldier and cowboy within nodded smugly at the challenge.

A nonsensical, prideful refrain began in his mind and grew louder with every step she took in his direction. *My lady. My lady. My lady.*

She stopped within arm's reach, and he reminded himself not to pull her in close. Josi wasn't his girlfriend. She was his friend-friend, and also his boss.

Why did that last thought suddenly have as much appeal as those motorcycle boots?

Mercy.

"You hate the look?" she asked, guessing incorrectly. "It's what I looked like when I spent time with that group. It's what all the women at the bonfire will look like too."

He seriously doubted that.

"I can't show up looking all fresh-faced and wholesome," she continued. "They'll accuse me of forgetting who I am and where I'm from. They might even say I think I'm better than them now. Then they'll run me off." She waved a hand between them.

Lincoln caught her wrist and towed her closer despite

himself. "Josi. You look like a badass, and I couldn't care less what anyone else thinks or looks like tonight. You shouldn't either."

Her eyes widened, then her shiny red lips turned up in a smile. "Yeah?"

He forced his gaze back to her eyes. "Yeah."

"You don't hate all this?" she asked, glancing down at herself without making any effort to escape his hold. "I thought you'd scoff. Miss the wholesome girl you know."

"I don't care what you wear or don't wear," he said, the words too sharp, his voice too low.

Josi's expression fell, and she stepped back.

His grip tightened. "That's not what I meant."

She pulled free of his grip and headed for the passenger door. "Yeah? What'd you mean then?"

They locked gazes across the hood of his truck, under the thin light of a new moon.

"I meant I like you as you are," he said. "The package that comes in doesn't matter." He yanked open his door and climbed inside, hating his inability to say the right thing at the right time.

The Beaumonts had four congenial brothers. Two lovable parents. And him. The uptight, prickly one. He couldn't even blame his personality on trauma. He'd been born without a need to aspire or impress, and that had served him fine until today.

Lincoln started the truck. He didn't need to look at Josi to know her eyes were on him. He knew better than to make another attempt to explain himself. That would only make things worse. So he shifted into gear and pointed them down the driveway. "Where are we going?"

"Potter's field."

He grunted. Not a place he wanted to be tonight. Too far

from town. From the police and hospitals. No one doing anything good would be there after dark.

"You know it?" Josi asked.

"The abandoned farmhouse where the road ends?"

"That's the place." Her voice hitched with surprise, but he kept his attention on the road. "Have you ever been there?"

"In high school," he said. Those days were before Josi's time there, no doubt. He'd never been so thankful for their five-year age difference. Growing up on a ranch for troubled teens, where he and his brothers were supposed to be shining examples, had led him to a life of rebellion. He'd done a number of things he wasn't particularly proud of. Those same experiences had made him an excellent fighter. The skills had since proven useful more times than he cared to count. The military had further fine-tuned his abilities until his hands alone were deadly. He'd never use them that way. But hand-to-hand combat had proven an incredible stress reducer. It was just difficult to find anyone willing to spar.

Lincoln shot a pointed look at Josi, who continued to scrutinize him. "What?"

"I never pegged you as a partier, that's all."

He ignored the comment, having no idea what to say in response.

"Lots of people, loud music, impromptu brawling," she said. "You had to hate it. Why'd you go?"

"I liked the brawling."

She laughed, then quickly quieted. "So you were like this before?"

"Before the military?" he asked. "Yeah. This is just…me."

"Interesting."

He looked at her again, prepared to voice the thing she

wouldn't say. "You thought I was like my brothers, and being a prisoner of war made me this way?"

"Couldn't have helped," she said.

His lips quirked with humor at her tone. He smashed them flat.

"Why do you do that?" she asked. "You fight every smile that tries to grace your face. What exactly do you think will happen if someone sees you have more than one mood?"

"I don't know," he said, lacing the words with sarcasm. "They'll probably keep talking to me."

She grinned. "Like me."

"No. Not like you." He frowned, sliding into comfortable territory as they glided along the winding ribbon of road. "You keep talking to me no matter how I behave. I've never understood why."

"Maybe I like you as you are too," she said. "Regardless of the packaging." Her eyes danced with delight as she sent his previous words back to him.

Lincoln refocused on the road.

The old farmhouse appeared a few minutes later, surrounded by trucks and partygoers. Shadows cloaked the porch and yard, while an inky dome of endless starlight shone overhead. Out back, a raging bonfire blazed in the field.

He backed into the grass, close enough to escape in a hurry if needed, and already pointing toward the road. He met Josi on her side of the truck.

She stared up at him, expectant. "I appreciate how gentlemanly you are, but this crowd will see any physical distance as a lack of interest on your part or mine. That will translate into an invitation for someone else to cut in. I don't like to fight, and I don't think you should. So if you're mine for the night, we're going to have to act like it."

His eyes narrowed. "What?"

"Permission to cling?" she asked, eyebrows rising in challenge.

He opened his arms in answer, and Josi stepped up. One narrow arm curved around his back, and she molded her body to his side. When he returned the gesture, pulling her in tight, she moved his palm onto her backside.

"Okay," she said. "Let's see what we can learn."

The old farmhouse was in worse shape than he remembered, which was saying a lot. The home's white paint had nearly worn off, exposing weathered boards. The front porch had sunk in one corner, and layers of spray paint coated the open door. A deep bass sound rumbled from within. A crush of bodies filled the interior.

Josi stepped away when they reached the threshold.

A chill rushed over his skin in her absence.

She pulled his hands onto her waist as she threaded her way into the crowd. Faces turned in their direction, some smiling, others clearly stunned. Josi greeted everyone warmly. Most looked at him as if he smelled bad.

Hopefully no one would want to fight. Hurting the partygoers probably wouldn't win them any help.

"Have you seen Tara?" Josi asked, repeatedly projecting her voice above the music, a mix of country and classic rock.

Each little clutch of people shook their heads, and Josi moved on.

When they reached the kitchen, a group of presumably underage partygoers stilled and stared. A game resembling beer pong had been set up on a table made of plywood and sawhorses.

Josi addressed the group.

"Ask Brady," a glassy-eyed young woman suggested, swinging an arm toward the backyard.

"Thanks."

When they reached the back porch, she released Lincoln. "You should wait here while I talk to Brady. I won't be long."

"That's not a good—"

She shook her head. "He's a friend. See that old Jeep? The man standing in the back?"

Lincoln scanned the darkened field. A Wrangler, at least five years his senior, was parked near an impressive bonfire. The Jeep was topless, roll bars exposed, and a beefy man closer to his age than hers stood inside, holding court from his throne.

A half-dozen other vehicles circled the fire, headlights or tailgates pointed at the flames.

"That's Brady," she said. "Give me a few minutes. You can see me from here."

"What about our lack of contact being an invitation?" he asked, imagining the number of men she would attract on her way across the field.

She smiled gently. "I'll set them straight when I get back." Rising onto her toes, she dug her fingers into his hair and slid her mouth against his cheek until it reached his ear. "Kiss me," she whispered. "My neck or cheek is fine. As long as whoever sees believes it."

She lowered and looked at him, eyes heavy lidded and gaze falling to his mouth. "If that's too much we can just—"

Lincoln's mouth was on her before she finished speaking. He drew her against him with hungry arms, pressing their bodies tight.

A tiny gasp escaped her lips, and he swallowed it, licking into her as he curled long fingers in her hair.

Josi returned the kiss with fervency, her sweet tongue sliding against his in delicious, tantalizing waves.

When she finally pulled back, expression wild and eyes dazed, he longed to toss her over one shoulder and leave the party behind. "Was that okay?" he asked, her befuddled expression failing to clear. He hadn't meant to get carried away, but damn, everything about Josi had felt so good.

She wet her lips and nodded. "Mmm-hmm."

"Did you ever date this Brady?" he asked, hating the senseless jealousy taking shape.

"Never."

Lincoln smiled. "Good, because he's watching." Along with everyone else.

Josi ran a fingertip over Lincoln's bottom lip. "I like when you smile," she said, clearly unbothered by their hot public display. "Especially when it's just for me."

If she only knew the things he'd do eagerly and repeatedly just for her.

Josi strutted away, chin high and shoulders back, a satisfied, prideful expression on her pretty face.

He tracked her with his gaze until she reached the Wrangler.

A mammoth-sized man jumped down, making her and everyone else appear tiny in his presence. Then, Josi leaped into his arms.

JOSI'S HEART HAMMERED as she clung to her one-time foster brother and lifelong guardian. He'd been the oldest kid in her first foster home, and he'd protected her from their handsy caretaker. After that, Brady had quickly become her best friend. He'd kept tabs on her, even after he'd aged out of the system, and their peers had respected his warning. As a result, she'd barely dated. Either the interested guys weren't up to Brady's standards, or they were too intimidated by him to give things a try. In hindsight, she appreciated his interference. Most of the guys on her radar had been trouble. Warning her away from them had probably saved her a lot of heartache. Brady, it seemed, had been saving her, in one way or another, for most of her life. For that, she owed him the world.

"I can't believe you're here," he said, swinging her in his arms.

"It's so good to see you," she said, eventually finding the ground with her tiptoes.

Brady released her and set his palms against the sides of her face, the way he had when she'd been lost to a panic attack. "You're just as beautiful as I remember."

"You too."

He dropped his hands to hers then raised one of her arms above her head and twirled her. "I take that back," he said when she stopped turning. "You look better than before. Healthier. Rested. Happy. Are you still at the Beaumont Ranch?"

"I am," she said, a rush of pride in her chest. Apparently he hadn't heard the announcement on the radio. Maybe the gunman hadn't either. "They made me the stable manager," she said proudly. "I take care of the horses and the riding schedule."

He crossed his arms and eyed her like the proud father or brother she'd never really had. "I never doubted that you'd be okay."

"I guess time really does change everything."

He cast his gaze around the field. "Not everything."

"Well, you're still the king, I see." She forced a brighter smile.

"Something like that." His attention slipped away, fixing on something in the distance.

Josi tracked his line of sight, then grabbed his arm before he did anything rash. "No. Hey. That's my boyfriend. He's with me."

"I saw," he said, one side of his mouth lifting in a mischievous smile. "Looks like a cop."

She laughed. "He's not a cop. He's just been in a bad mood all his life."

Brady dragged his eyes to hers, uncertainty etched on his brow. "What's his name?"

"Lincoln Beaumont."

Brady barked a laugh, stance and limbs loosening. "Dating the boss?"

"No." She bristled. "I'm his boss. He's a ranch hand."

Brady considered that a moment, then nodded, apparently in approval. "Is he good to you?"

"Very." Memories of their unexpected kiss burst into her mind and heat coiled in her core. She wasn't really dating Lincoln, but he'd never been anything other than good to her, and she was certain the treatment only got better when his whole heart was involved.

Voices rose near the fire, forcing Josi to double down on her quest.

If a fight broke out, Brady would have to leave her, and he might not have time for her later. "Before I go," she said, pulling his attention away from the disagreement. "Have you seen Tara lately? She called me last night from the Bayside Motel, but I can't reach her now."

He turned back to her, temporarily ignoring the ruckus. "What was she doing there?"

"I don't know. I went to pick her up, but someone else

was there. He took a shot at her and she ran. Any idea who'd want to hurt her?"

Brady scanned Josi's face, then took another look in Lincoln's direction. "I'm not sure. I've heard whispering to suggest she was mixed up in something she shouldn't have been involved in, but no one's big on details. You remember."

She did. "Any guess about what it could be?"

He shook his head, eyes back on the fire. "Sounds like real trouble if there were shots fired."

"True."

"Is your new man in the military?" Brady asked, effectively changing the subject.

"He was." She turned to look at Lincoln.

"Ranger? Special Ops?"

"Ranger," she said. "How'd you know?"

"My brother was a ranger. I'd recognize that stance and that gaze anywhere." He chuckled. "Look at the way he's watching you. He's clearly in love. Does he have the tattoo?"

"I don't think so," she said. "What tattoo?" She'd never noticed a tattoo on Lincoln, but now that the idea had been planted, she loved it.

"They all get one," Brady said. "People don't push themselves into that league and not write it on their body." His expression turned disbelieving. "Wait. How long have you been seeing this guy?"

She stilled, realizing her error. If she and Lincoln were in love, she'd know about all his tattoos. "We're taking things slow."

Brady raised his eyebrows. "Well, I hope your guy's temper is better than my brother's. If he ever hurts you—"

"He wouldn't." Josi turned to examine Lincoln from a distance. As promised, his attention was fixed on her.

A woman screamed as the nearby argument broke into a fight.

"That's my cue," Brady said. "Tell your man to take you home. It's been good to see you, Josi, but this place isn't for you anymore. Do yourself a favor and stay away."

Chapter Seven

Lincoln met Josi at the bottom of the porch steps and hooked an arm around her waist. "Let's go."

The fight near the fire was going strong, and the man she'd been talking to was wholly distracted. So he probably hadn't noticed the handful of men who'd broken away from the pack. The group had moved toward the house behind Josi. They kept their distance, but Lincoln's instincts told him it was time to leave.

She checked over her shoulder, then took his hand. Together, they hustled around the side of the house, across the grass to his waiting truck.

He unlocked the vehicle with his fob as they approached. "Climb over."

She bolted through the driver's side and over the console without question. Clearly, she sensed trouble too.

Lincoln locked the doors as he settled behind the wheel, checking the darkened yard for signs of the men who'd been following. "You okay?" He started the engine and pulled onto the road.

"Yeah. You?"

Lincoln checked the rearview mirror, thankful for the darkness. Maybe his sixth sense was on the fritz after his panic attack that afternoon. Maybe he'd developed paranoia.

He rolled his shoulders and stretched his fingers against the steering wheel. "Better now. Did you get what you went for?"

Josi released a long, slow breath. "I did, but not because anyone wanted to volunteer information. The overwhelming lack of input tells me something's up. Maybe they no longer trust me, because I've become an outsider."

"Or?"

"Or there's a big problem no one wants to be involved in or caught talking about."

A set of distant headlights drew his attention to the rearview mirror as they motored away.

Josi turned to peer through the back window.

"Tell me more about the big guy on the Jeep," he said, determined not to overreact to the other vehicle without reason.

"He's kind of their king." She laughed softly. "More like a convoluted big-brother figure. They all respect him, and he does what he can to help them. He looked out for me all my life, but I haven't even called him since moving to the ranch. Apparently this was our goodbye."

"Goodbye?"

She took a shaky breath. "He told me I don't belong here anymore."

Lincoln set his hand on hers and offered a gentle squeeze as they rounded a wide curve.

Behind them, two other vehicles had joined the first.

Multiple people leaving a party together wasn't unusual. He might've convinced himself of the possibility if the trio wasn't gaining on him.

"Looks like we might have trouble," he said, releasing her hand in favor of gripping the steering wheel.

Josi tugged her seat belt, adjusting it across her hips as if preparing for a crash. "You've got this," she said, voice level and steady. "Last time someone followed us, we were downtown. You had to deal with oncoming vehicles, pedestrians, buildings and speed limits. This is just endless fields and open road. Plus, I've seen what you and this truck can do."

Lincoln certainly hoped she was right.

Losing a few cars on roads he'd been driving since long before he had a license wouldn't be nearly as tough as dropping a tail in traffic. And his truck was a beast. Even if the cars could catch him, they couldn't hurt his ride. His passenger was the real concern. Whatever happened, he needed to keep her safe.

Behind him, the vehicles raced forward, their collective engine growls making the world outside seem to vibrate. A small yellow hatchback darted into the opposite lane, then pulled in front of the truck, causing Lincoln to swerve. His passenger-side tires hit the loose rocks along the narrow shoulder, and the pickup wobbled before returning to the pavement. The second car moved into position at their side, facing off with nonexistent traffic in the opposite lane. The third vehicle, a dark SUV, charged forward and nudged his rear bumper gently.

Lincoln released his wheel with one hand and tapped his dashboard. Whatever happened now wouldn't be good. "Call 911."

"Calling 911," the truck repeated.

Josi craned her neck for a better look at the situation. "What do we do?"

"Stay calm," he said.

"Oh, sure." She watched the tiny hatchback, perplexed and more than a little concerned. What could the goal possibly be? Lincoln's truck was twice the size of either car and big enough to easily crush the SUV.

She could only hope the gunman wasn't in one of the rides.

Lincoln adjusted his mirrors and set his jaw. "This exercise is probably meant for intimidation."

"Well, it's working on me," she said.

The SUV behind them lurched forward again, its headlights stealing her sight and probably Lincoln's, though he didn't show it.

He relayed the details of their situation and location to the dispatcher who'd answered his call, then cited the makes and models of all three vehicles. "No rear plate on the hatchback ahead of us," he said. "No front plates on the other two."

The three cars seemed to adjust their speeds in sync, drawing closer to Lincoln's truck, closing in on them as they approached the next curve.

"They're going to run us off the road," she said, suddenly terrified for new reasons. If they got Lincoln out of the truck, things would get ugly fast. Three on one wasn't a fair fight, and one thing the people from her past didn't care about was being fair. Also, they loved to send messages.

"Doubtful," Lincoln said. "You still doing okay?"

She made a soft, noncommittal sound, certain it wasn't time to tell the whole truth. "You?"

"I'm good," he said, expression flat and gaze hard. The muscles in his arms flexed and released with each micro movement of the wheel. "Hold tight."

Before she could ask for clarification, Lincoln jerked the wheel in a sharp one-two move, cracking against the little car beside them.

The car spun out, tossing loose dirt and gravel into the

air as it left the road and smacked its back corner panel against a tree.

Josi's body jolted. Her head flopped from side to side as Lincoln recentered his truck in the lane.

"Are you still there?" the voice from the speakers queried.

"We're here," Josi called.

"What happened?"

"One of the cars left the road."

"Are they injured?" the dispatcher asked.

"I don't know. There's still someone behind us and another car—" She screamed as the truck's engine revved suddenly and the pickup dove ahead. Lincoln smacked into the rear bumper of the hatchback, the way the SUV had done to them.

The hatchback swerved wildly in response. Its headlights cut paths across the center lines before the driver overcorrected and peeled along the narrow shoulder.

Lincoln followed, the truck's big tires eating up the dirt and rocks. He hit the car again, and it shot forward, leaving patches of black on the asphalt as the driver struggled to regain control before the next curve.

Brake lights painted the night in red. A moment later, the car tore headlong into a shallow culvert at the roadside.

"Two down," Lincoln stated flatly, picking up speed in the obstacle's absence. His hard gaze flickered to the dashboard and ongoing call. "Where are those officers you promised?"

"On the way," the dispatcher returned dryly. "I'm sending a pair of ambulances now as well. Can you head toward town?"

Josi frowned as confusion set in. "Do you know one another?"

"Everybody knows Lincoln Beaumont," the older man barked. "We just thought his trouble-making days were over."

"I'm the victim," Lincoln said, a note of amusement in his otherwise flat tone.

"I've heard that somewhere before. Oh, yeah," the other man said. "From you."

Lincoln grinned. "You think if I slam my brakes he'll fly right by me?"

"Do not pull any of that *Top Gun* mess on me right now," the dispatcher complained. "There's a cruiser less than two minutes out and another pair en route. Just keep driving. Medics will follow."

The SUV ignited its high beams, and Lincoln flipped his rearview mirror, returning the light to them.

A gunshot sounded, and Lincoln steered the pickup into the other lane.

"Shooter," he stated, picking up speed once more.

In the distance, headlights and emergency flashers appeared.

"I see the cruiser!" Josi called.

Her body jerked and bent forward as the truck slowed suddenly, and the SUV arrived beside her door.

Lincoln smacked the truck against the smaller ride, just as he had the first car, forcing the SUV onto the shoulder. A mass of trees up ahead would soon stop the other vehicle, if they didn't give up on their own.

Sirens burst through the night as the cruiser barreled nearer, and Lincoln eased away from the SUV.

Josi's shoulders slammed against the door at her side as he rammed into the SUV once more.

Then the other vehicle began to roll.

"What's happening?" the man on the other end of the line demanded.

Josi struggled to breathe as the SUV rocked to a stop, tires in the air.

The cruiser angled across the road, stopping Lincoln's truck with a final whoop of the siren.

He shifted into Park and turned to her. "You okay?"

"No." Her heart beat ruthlessly against her chest. An SUV was on its roof in the field at their side. And a mass of emergency vehicles were eating up the night in their direction.

"I wouldn't have done that if he hadn't taken a shot at us," Lincoln said. "If he'd hit one of my tires at that speed, or worse, gotten a shot through the back window and into one of us—" He shook his head slowly.

Her lips finally parted, but her voice didn't come. Her thoughts were muddled, and her mouth went dry.

"Take deep breaths," Lincoln said. "I'll be right back." He climbed out and met the officer outside the first cruiser. He pointed to the road behind them, presumably relaying details about the other vehicles involved.

He returned quickly, as promised, then fished a bag from behind his seat. He unearthed a bottle of water and passed it into her hands. "Drink."

She took several long gulps before her thoughts began to clear.

"You're probably experiencing mild shock." Lincoln returned to his seat, closing the door behind him and shutting out the night. "I didn't mean to scare you."

He leaned forward, cool green eyes locked on hers, and her racing heart began to thud for new reasons. "Josi." His big hands found her face. He cupped her jaw and caressed her cheek with the pads of his thumbs. "You're okay, and I'm right here."

She unfastened her seat belt with trembling hands, causing him to release her. Then she threw herself across the console and wrapped her arms around his neck. "Thank you."

Chapter Eight

Lincoln stiffened as Josi's arms came around him. Then, on instinct, he hugged her back.

She pressed her cheek to his chest, shuddered breaths rattling her small frame.

The scent of her, warm vanilla and coconuts, encased him. Her need for safety and reassurance broke his heart, as did the fact his driving was at least part of the cause for her distress. Yet she'd turned to him for comfort, and it was nearly his undoing.

"Hey, you're okay," he whispered, lowering his mouth to her ear. Sounds of incoming sirens and loud male voices outside his window couldn't hold his attention, not with Josi in his arms. "Everyone's okay."

His hammering heart and racing thoughts slowed and tunneled until everything else fell away. "Shh." He stroked her hair and gathered her closer. "I didn't mean to scare you." He hadn't meant to do anything except keep her safe. Until the final driver had taken a shot at them, he'd been careful not to use more aggression than necessary to remove the offending vehicles as threats. But an armed assailant couldn't be allowed.

A loud knock against the glass beside his head sent Josi away like an electric shock.

Her eyes widened as they took in whoever had ruined his moment.

He gritted his teeth before turning to glare at Finn. "Hello, Detective." He powered down his window, fighting the urge to bark at his brother for no good reason.

"How y'all doing tonight?" he asked somewhat casually, given the situation.

Lincoln climbed out and closed the door. "Any ID on the drivers?"

Finn smirked, unspeaking for an extended beat, then responded. "Nope, but that vehicle was reported stolen two nights ago. The owner's going to love knowing we found it. Probably not the part where it's standing on its roof, but sometimes we have to take the good with the bad. I don't suppose you know how it got like that?"

Lincoln glanced at the scuffed paint and dented front corner panel of his truck. "Hard to say. He took a shot at us, and a few seconds later he lost control."

"Mmm-hmm. That didn't exactly answer my question, but I expected something similar," Finn said. He sidestepped his older brother for a look through the still-open window. "How you doing, Josi? You hurt? I've got an extra ambulance on the way."

"I'm okay," she said, cheeks darkening as her gaze slipped to Lincoln.

A rush of warmth slid over him, and he rocked back on his heels. "Were the other drivers hurt?" Lincoln asked.

In the field at their side, EMTs and officers guided the SUV's driver onto the grass for an examination.

"We only found one other car," Finn said. "A yellow hatchback stuck in a little culvert about a half mile back. That guy's just upset about the damage to his car."

Josi left her seat and rounded the hood to Finn's side.

She slid under his arm in an easy side hug before moving to stand with Lincoln.

He bit the insides of his cheeks to stop a smile from forming when their coat sleeves touched. She'd never treated him like a sibling, but she was starting to treat him like more than a coworker or friend. And despite their agreement to pretend they were an item, everything about their kiss had felt very real.

"Any idea who these guys are or what they're up to?" Finn asked, gaze trailing a cruiser as it crept past them, an angry-looking guy in the back seat. Presumably the hatchback's driver.

Josi stared at the car, then switched her attention to the SUV's driver, now cuffed to a gurney and being lifted into an ambulance. "Their names are Carson and Willy. That's Willy."

Finn looked over his shoulder to the man in cuffs. "Last names?"

She shook her head. "No. We were never friends. They're part of a little crew."

"A gang?" he asked.

She shrugged. "Whatever you want to call them. I steered clear."

"What do they normally get up to?"

Josi leaned against Lincoln, and his arm rose instinctively to support her. "Nothing good."

Finn's gaze dropped to the point of physical contact between Lincoln and Josi.

"I have an idea about where you can find the driver who got away," Lincoln said. "It could tell us how this set of guys are connected." The thought had occurred to him before the chase began, then slipped away when things grew dicey on the road. "I saw tattoos on a few of the men at the party that looked a lot like the ones folks involved with that bare-knuckle fight club had."

Finn's normally easy expression fell into a scowl.

"I'd start at their gym, or wherever they're training now," Lincoln said.

The fight club had been one of the town's biggest stories a few years back. Lincoln had been overseas, but news had traveled to him via his family. The ring had been successfully dismantled following the death of a local man, barely older than Finn at the time, which had wholly upset their mother, who worried incessantly about everyone.

Lincoln couldn't recall the young man's name.

"Tara had a direct connection to that club," Finn said, his voice oddly tight, eyes locked with Josi's.

Josi blinked tear-filled eyes, a soft gasp leaving her lips.

"You okay?" Lincoln asked, angling for a look at her paling face. Was she in shock? Was she going to pass out? "Let's talk to the medic at that ambulance. Ask him for an evaluation."

"No. I'm—" She shook her head and straightened. "Finn's right."

"Tara's brother—" She swallowed hard, limbs going stiff. "Marcus made ends meet by fighting for them."

Lincoln looked from his brother to Josi. They seemed to know something he didn't. "Where is he now?" Lincoln asked.

"Dead." Her voice cracked on the single word.

The brothers locked gazes and understanding passed between them. Tara's brother was the man who'd died. The reason Finn had been able to shut down the operation once and for all.

The ugly puzzle pieces shifted a little closer to one another in Lincoln's mind. "Was Tara part of that crowd?"

"She knew them, but they weren't friends. They're older than us. And her brother did what he could to keep her away from trouble."

"Like a good brother would," Finn said.

Josi nodded. "He was the best."

"Any chance she held a grudge?" Lincoln asked. "Maybe she got some dirt on them, blamed someone else for their part in his death?"

Josi swung weary eyes from him to Finn, then back. "All I know is there's nothing she wouldn't do for Marcus."

AN HOUR LATER, Josi carried a glass of iced water from Lincoln's small kitchen island to the simple brown couch in his living area. She couldn't help marveling at the contrast between her place and his. Lincoln's cabin was identical to hers in layout. The decor, however, couldn't have been more different. Where her rooms overflowed with frills and fluff, hosting every shabby-chic thrift-store find that had crossed her path, Lincoln had stuck to minimalism. If her home was adorably cluttered, his was severely spotless.

She lowered onto the sofa's edge a few steps later, her thoughts a tangled mess. "I really hope we're wrong about the fight club."

"Me too," Lincoln said, taking a seat two cushions away. "It's a hunch based on tattoos. Could easily turn out to be nothing. Finn will know more soon."

She bit her bottom lip, overwhelmed by the entirety of her day. She was accustomed to being physically exhausted at this hour, but it'd been a long while since she'd been so emotionally and mentally drained.

Despite the devotion of her time and best efforts, Tara was still missing.

"How are you holding up?" Lincoln asked. He hooked one sock-covered foot over the opposite knee and leaned back against the worn couch. The picture of ease.

"I'm processing."

"Want to talk about it?"

She glanced at him, noticing the cream throw pillow between them, and a matching blanket over the back of the couch. Upgrades to the otherwise utilitarian furniture. Gifts from his mother, no doubt. The plush area rug beneath his coffee table was likely from her as well.

"We'll find your friend," Lincoln said.

Josi swallowed a lump of unexpected emotion. "I'm really worried about her."

"We all are."

The kind words choked Josi further, because she knew they were true. The Beaumonts didn't need to know someone to love them or want them safe.

"Your friend, Brady, didn't have any insight?" he asked, eyebrows rising as he delivered the question.

"No." Though it was hard to believe whatever caused a gunman to take a shot at Tara would fly under Brady's radar. He and Tara hadn't been close, but the goons who'd chased Lincoln's truck had been at the party. Brady had to have known them somehow. "Nothing that he shared," she amended, suddenly unsure of her relationship to the guy who'd always looked out for her before.

"What did you talk about?"

Josi set her glass on the coffee table and pulled a pillow into her lap. "You, a little."

A muscle along Lincoln's jaw clenched and flexed. "How'd that go?"

"Not great," she admitted. "He could tell you were former military. Then he guessed you as a ranger. His brother was a ranger too."

Lincoln's body stiffened the way it always did at the mention of his time in service.

"He saw you watching me and thought you looked like you were in love." She smiled to ease the tension. "He also hoped your temper wasn't as bad as his brother's—for my safety, I guess."

"I would never hurt you." The words were out of his mouth before she stopped speaking.

Josi stilled. "I know."

The tension she often felt between them suddenly increased, and Josi looked away. "You know I grew up in foster care," she said, turning the conversation to herself.

Lincoln always appeared uncomfortable when he was the topic of discussion. He hadn't asked, but since they were spending so much time together, maybe he'd like to know more about her. She'd certainly like to know more about him.

He lowered his chin. "I do."

"My mom was an addict, and I don't know anything about my dad," she said, supposing the information was relevant, given their current circumstance. "My mom's parents were flat broke and long tired of her drama by the time I was born. They were too old, too poor and too exhausted from raising Mom to step up for me when she failed. If they had, it would've meant starting all over as parents for them, and she'd have been in their lives another eighteen years. So they opted out, and every time the courts pulled me from Mom's care, I bounced around the system until they put me back. I didn't get a permanent foster placement when I was young, because she was too stubborn to give me up and not quite bad enough to lose me completely."

Josi took a slow, steadying breath and pushed on. Humiliating and humbling as it was, Lincoln deserved to hear it and know who he was protecting. "I stayed with a few nice families at first, but placements were harder to find by middle school, and I started running away. I knew Mom would pull me back into her life at the next opportunity, and I didn't want to be around when that happened. As a result, I missed a lot of school, got into fights, shoplifted food when I was hungry. Spent a little time in juvenile correction centers for that. Eventually, Mom overdosed and died. I was sixteen. No one wanted to bring a kid that age, with my history, into their nice little home. So they didn't."

Lincoln leaned forward, resting his forearms on his thighs, attention rapt. "Go on," he urged.

"With my mom gone, I returned to school. I took summer classes to make up for failed or incomplete courses. I worked hard and graduated on time. I still got in a little trouble, and I lived in my car for a while, but I survived. And I cobbled together a makeshift family of other teens in similar situations. We supported one another." She grinned despite herself. Things had been rough, but she'd done well, and life had gotten much better. "Then your family brought me here when social workers caught up with me right before my eighteenth birthday. Your folks said I could stay as long as I needed to get on my feet."

He let his lips turn up in a lazy half smile. "How's that going for you?"

"Well..." She dragged her gaze away from his mouth and was immediately drawn in by those remarkable moss-green eyes. "They even let me work with their most difficult son."

Lincoln released a small snort. "There's a price for everything."

"Now, I have a question for you."

"I didn't ask you anything," he argued.

"You wanted to," she said, hoping she was right.

Josi wet her lips and let her eager gaze slide over his arms. "Do you have a tattoo that says you're a ranger?"

His Adam's apple bobbed, and her attention moved to the long, tan column of his throat. "Why?"

"Brady said you'd have one, and I almost blew our cover when I said I didn't know."

Lincoln sat taller, searching her face for something she couldn't guess. "How'd you explain that?"

"I told him we're taking things slow." Her chest and cheeks heated at the implication she would see him without his clothes soon.

In her fake relationship.

Lincoln reached behind his head without breaking eye contact. He gathered the material of his shirt in both hands and lifted, revealing every amazing inch of tanned skin from waist to shoulders. He balled the shirt in one fist after it cleared his head, then he sat half-naked for her inspection.

She wanted to wave a hand and tell him he didn't need to do that. That he shouldn't start removing his clothes. Or she'd start removing hers, and who knew what might happen then? But her tongue stood still, and her lips didn't move. She barely remembered to breathe. The hard, flat expanse of his chest rose and fell at a steady, confident pace. His deeply defined abdominals begged for her touch. She could feel the heat of his body, could imagine his warm, soft skin against her fingertips.

A dark, puckered scar along his tapered side pushed her thoughts from sexy to concerned.

"What happened?" she asked, removing the distance between them. Her hand lifted, then returned to her lap. For a moment, she'd considered touching the marred skin, hating that he'd been so obviously hurt.

Then she remembered the game they played as boyfriend and girlfriend was limited to time spent outside these walls.

"I was shot," he said. "When my team was taken. I wish I could say that was the worst day."

Her gaze jumped to his. "I'm so sorry." For him. For his teammates. Their families.

Her gut wrenched, and she struggled to school her expression.

"My ranger tattoo is on my back." He shifted away from her, turning to expose his more severely scarred back.

Jagged ropes of raised skin crisscrossed his spine and stretched toward his sides in every direction. Cuts, she assumed, maybe lashes. And burns.

Her world tilted as evidence of what she'd heard from Beaumont family whispers became irrevocably clear.

Lincoln had endured torture.

She batted away unshed tears, refocused on the mission at hand.

In the midst of numerous scars, two black bands curled like banners in the wind. Cutouts in the ink formed letters. The letters made a single word on each line. Airborne. Ranger.

Simple, direct and to the point, she thought. Exactly like the man who'd chosen it.

"You were airborne," she said. "I didn't know." Her hands lifted to his skin. "May I?"

He shrugged, easily understanding the request.

Josi trailed her fingertips across the words, grazing lightly at first, then exploring more thoroughly when he relaxed against her touch. Her breath caught at the small gesture, and she bit her lip, fighting a smile.

"You know some of the details about what I went through," he said, voice low but steady. "My family likes to talk."

"They lean on one another," she said. "They support and comfort each other. It's more than just talk."

"So you know," he repeated. "About what happened to me."

No one had given her details, but she'd understood what a failed recovery mission meant. Knew that when the team went missing, the reason wasn't good. And she'd put the rest together on her own when Lincoln had been the only one rescued many months later when a second team had been deployed. "I know enough."

Lincoln was silent for a long while as her fingertips trailed paths over his warm skin and tragic scars. "We were supposed to return together, with one addition, the soldier we went to save."

He shivered when the tips of fingers skimmed the lengths of his sides.

"Sorry, I just—" Hadn't stopped touching him since the moment she'd begun.

She'd gotten carried away and forgotten herself for a moment.

Lincoln turned to face her, his expression unprecedentedly vulnerable. "Then you know I'm broken," he said. "I was too messed up to keep fighting, so they sent me home. And I'm too wrecked to be a decent civilian, which is the reason I still live on the ranch and work in the barn. I'm not sure where I belong, so I just try to stay busy and be useful when I can."

Josi felt her breaking heart snap, and protectiveness rose inside her. "I live here and work in the barn too, you know."

His lips quirked, fighting the small smile she loved.

"For what it's worth," she said, opening her arms and leaning in to hug him. "I think you are exactly where you belong."

Chapter Nine

Lincoln woke to the feel of warm skin against him and strands of soft, coconut-scented hair across his cheek. His eyelids flashed open to find Josi in his arms. Apparently they'd fallen asleep on the couch, then somehow stretched out to lie on their sides. Her body nestled against his. Her back to his chest, each of them facing the window across the room. He'd curled an arm over her, and she held on to it like a life raft, even in sleep.

His lids drifted shut as he recalled the long hours they'd spent together, both tired, but neither willing to call it a night. They'd stubbornly watched movies until the wee hours, talking about everything and nothing, missing the entirety of what happened on-screen.

He'd learned more about her past, devouring all the bits and pieces she'd been willing to share. And he'd told her things he rarely told anyone. About growing up on the ranch. Getting in trouble frequently. And his unending love of the seaside. They'd even made plans to ride horses on the beach after Tara was home safely. Despite all the reasons they had to be uneasy and stressed out, they'd laughed. Everything about the night had felt easy and right.

Josi was exactly who she seemed to be. Genuine and true. Vulnerable but tough. Kind to her very core. She was

the type of woman he'd always hoped to meet. The sort
who wouldn't judge him for his damage. Or leave him because of it.

His eyes opened once more.

Thoughts like those deeply underscored the reason he
shouldn't be curled up with her. Even if Lincoln's broken
pieces didn't bother her, Josi deserved so much more. Not
to mention his family would probably kill him for thinking any of the things that had been on his mind where Josi
was concerned.

He rose onto his elbow, angling for a look at the nearest
clock. The golden hue of a rising sun beyond the window
suggested they'd be late for breakfast and work, if they
didn't get moving soon.

Josi moaned, and his mind formed instant images and
mental lists of all the ways he could incite similar sounds.

He needed distance. Immediately.

Lincoln held his breath and tried to slip away. He could
make a run for the farmhouse. The cool morning air would
bring him back to reality.

She'd be safe until he returned, and he could bring breakfast. A win-win.

Josi rocked back as he tried to escape, pressing him
against the couch with her tight, round backside.

Lincoln's body responded naturally, instinctively, and he
grimaced as she rolled to face him on the narrow cushions.

"Good morning," she said, raising sleepy eyes up to his.
"Why are you frowning already? Weren't you able to sleep?"

Her words stalled his panic and redirected his thoughts.
"Actually, I did," he said, mystified. "And I never sleep."
Not really. Not for more than an hour or so at a time. He
hadn't in years, and he'd given up hope that he ever would
again. But last night he'd slept soundly with her in his arms.

"Is something else bothering you?" she asked, settling one small palm on his T-shirt, just above his heart.

Could she feel the erratic beating?

"Hungry," he said, hoping she'd believe the lie. "Do you want breakfast?" He needed a change of subject almost as much as he needed to put some space between them. He couldn't think clearly with her body touching his from thigh to chest.

His gaze dropped several inches at the thought.

She'd changed into a tank top and pajama pants before bed.

Last night he'd done his best not to notice the way the shirt clung to her lean form, accentuating her curves. But now, pressed against him the way she was...

He met her eyes once more. He could feel the shape of her, and she could, no doubt, feel the shape of him.

A heavy knock against the door made him spring to his feet.

"Lincoln," his mom called. "I brought breakfast. Everyone awake in there?"

Lincoln crossed the room in a rush, thankful for the escape and anxious to prove he wasn't doing any of the things he desperately wanted to do.

JOSI ANGLED HERSELF UPRIGHT, dragging her fingers through tangled, sleep-mussed hair. Embarrassment heated her cheeks as she straightened her shirt and stood. She'd thought Lincoln had let down his guard enough last night for them to be comfortable now. Maybe even friends. The way he'd held her while they'd slept, and the way his body had responded to hers after she woke, made her think that maybe she wasn't alone in her feelings for him.

Then his mother had arrived, and he'd shot across

the room to greet her, unable to escape Josi fast enough. Clearly, she'd misread everything, and he was probably horrified, knowing she'd made those assumptions. Hence his wild dash to the door.

"Morning, Josi," Mrs. Beaumont said, bustling past the couch to the kitchen. She'd pulled her salt-and-pepper hair into a low ponytail, and donned a coat to protect her from the weather. Her knowing smile made Josi squirm. "I made cheesy scrambled eggs with diced garden veggies, and I packed a few biscuits with jam and honey. There's fresh fruit at the farmhouse and plenty of coffee, but I wasn't sure if y'all plan to be out and about today." She set a thermal casserole-shaped tote on the counter and unearthed the condiments from a small handled bag.

"Thank you," Josi said. "Everything smells delicious. I'm sure we'll still come around your place in a bit. You know how much I hate to miss a proper Beaumont breakfast."

Mrs. Beaumont grinned, visibly pleased with Josi's response. "Good. And for what it's worth, I know all about what happened last night," she added, tossing a pointed gaze at Lincoln. "No need for the both of you to look so guilty."

Josi stiffened as a dozen thoughts crammed into mind. What exactly had she seen? And how?

Did she know about their kiss?

"What are you talking about, Mama?" Lincoln asked, his tone a little sharp.

Mrs. Beaumont wrinkled her nose. "You must've known I'd hear. No thanks to either of you." She swung her attention to Josi, then back to Lincoln. "Y'all were chased by three cars and neither of you bothered to tell me."

"One of the drivers took a shot at us," Josi blurted, pulling her knees to her chest, and glad to look rattled for a much better reason.

"Goodness." Mrs. Beaumont pressed a palm to her collarbone, eyes wide. Maternal concern lined her pretty face. "No one told me that part. You'd better start the coffee, Lincoln."

He obeyed, casting a sideways glance at Josi on his way into the kitchen.

She hoped he didn't regret how much of his life he'd shared the night before, because she didn't want that to stop. Getting to know him and learning about his past had been wonderful and fun. Even if he didn't want her in the same way she wanted him, she couldn't bear to lose the new connection they'd formed.

"Any news on your friend?" Mrs. Beaumont asked, pulling Josi's attention away from Lincoln.

Shame slid up Josi's spine and across her cheeks. She hadn't even thought of her missing friend since waking in Lincoln's arms. What kind of person was she?

Tara's disappearance and well-being should've been the first things on her mind.

Lincoln leaned against the countertop as the coffee brewed. He rested big palms on either side of him, the usual scowl on his face. "Nothing yet," he said, answering his mother when Josi struggled for words. "But it's still early."

"You're right about that," Mrs. Beaumont agreed. "Finn's coming for breakfast at the house, so I can't stay. I've got sausage gravy cooking for the biscuits. Y'all eat up, and come over when you can. Hope everything else went okay."

Something in her tone made Lincoln narrow his eyes, and his mother's lips curled slightly in humor. She tucked away the expression before smiling politely at Josi and heading for the door. "I'll see myself out. Enjoy!"

Lincoln sighed deeply, then hung his head.

Josi grinned. Suddenly, despite the nonsensical feelings

of abandonment he'd caused by leaping from the couch, and a pinch of embarrassment over her hopeless crush, she began to laugh.

"What?"

"Your mama came to see if we were up to anything good," Josi said. "This meal delivery was a cover-up."

Lincoln's cheeks darkened slightly, but he didn't argue.

"She thinks there might be something going on between us," Josi teased, her tone low and scandalous.

"Seems that way," he said, then he turned his back on her to pour the coffee.

Not exactly the reaction she'd hoped for.

Chapter Ten

Lincoln returned from the shower as quickly as possible, only to find Josi missing and her cup of coffee abandoned on the countertop. His stomach tightened at the sight. Not because he thought she was in trouble, but because she'd been distant the moment he'd handed the drink to her. He'd been certain his mama was the cause, and he'd excused himself as quickly as possible to get cleaned up before starting the day. He'd hoped to return to a subject change.

Not an empty living room.

He reminded himself it was highly unlikely she'd been abducted from his cabin as he stuffed his feet into boots. There were few places in Marshal's Bluff safer than the ranch.

She'd probably decided to go home and get ready for her day as well.

He sent a text to confirm her whereabouts and safety.

Josi replied a moment later. As expected, she'd gone home to shower and change.

Lincoln pulled a wool-lined denim jacket from the hooks near his front door and ran a hand through his still-damp hair before heading out. The sun was bright in the sky, but there were enough clouds on the horizon to shake his hope of a full day without rain.

Green grass stretched to the horizon in all directions,

occasionally broken up by livestock, outbuildings, barns and farm hands. A group of men near the stables raised their arms in greeting.

Lincoln paused then slowly returned the gesture.

"Enjoy the time off," one man called. "Looks like the rain might hold out a while today."

"Thanks," Lincoln said, projecting his voice through the distance. "Will do."

Apparently, his mama had already sent folks to handle his job today and likely Josi's too. He hadn't missed the look in Mama's eyes as she'd surveyed him this morning, noticing everything he didn't want her to see, no doubt. And Josi had picked up on her intent.

It wasn't any wonder Josi had run off at the first opportunity.

Lincoln climbed the steps to her cabin and took a seat on the porch. When she came outside, they could walk to the farmhouse together and see if Finn had any updates to share.

In the meantime, he let his thoughts wander over the case and facts at hand. Tara was gone and someone didn't want Josi asking questions. Did the drivers who'd chased them have a personal stake in the other woman's disappearance, or had they been sent by someone else? And if so, who? Petey from the pawnshop? Maybe someone he'd told about Josi's recent visit? The number of people who'd seen her asking questions was rising fast. There'd been two younger guys with Petey and dozens of folks at the party. News always spread like wildfire in small communities, especially when it shouldn't, which created a town full of suspects.

The cabin door sucked open behind him, derailing his thoughts.

"Oh," Josi said. "I thought I'd meet you back at your cabin. Or at the farmhouse, if you'd already left."

Lincoln rose to his feet. "Hope you didn't mind me waiting."

She looked away. "No. I just needed to clean up a little. Get ready for whatever today will hold."

Josi's cheeks were rosy and her lips shone. She'd added something dark to her lashes and traded her pajama bottoms for black stretchy pants that clung to her like a second skin. The hooded sweatshirt she'd paired with them barely reached her waist, and memories of her perfect body curved against him earlier returned with a heavy smack.

"You're glaring," she said, voice a little sharp. "Are you upset because I left your cabin? I knew I'd be safe coming home to get ready."

"No," he said, matching her tone. "I was just thinking."

"About?" She crossed her arms and turned on him.

"You look nice."

Josi's expression went blank. Her shiny lips parted, and she blinked.

He refused to roll his eyes, rub his forehead, or otherwise give away the internal tirade his words had unleashed. It wasn't like him to go around complimenting women on their appearances. Especially not his boss. His girlfriend, of course, but Josi wasn't that, which made the whole thing akin to a catcall, albeit a polite one.

"Thank you," she said, shocking him back to the moment. "You look nice too. I wasn't sure about these pants. I'm accustomed to wearing jeans around the farm."

"We have the day off, it seems," he said, motioning to the men leading horses into the pasture. "So no dress code."

"Then the outfit's okay?" She lifted her arms and turned in a circle. The movement raised her cropped hoodie, revealing a glimpse of tanned skin above her waistband. The pants outlined every curve and contour of her lean, toned hips and legs.

"I like it," he said.

She smiled, and something flashed in her eyes.

He'd seen the look multiple times the night before. A mischievous glint that often came with her little challenges, teases or taunts. Last night he'd devoured them. He'd even suspected she was flirting. Was she flirting now?

"Lincoln," she said, stepping closer.

A small grunt escaped him in answer.

"We should probably talk about the fact we slept together."

Lincoln barked an unexpected laugh, and her smile split, revealing a full set of straight white teeth.

"Based on the look your mama gave," she continued, "and the fact Finn's on his way, speculation will probably be making its rounds soon. We should prepare ourselves."

"Agreed," he said, willing to prepare in whatever way she wanted, as long as she continued to look at him like that. "Suggestions?"

Josi took another step forward, then rose onto her toes and motioned him to lean toward her. "What if we gave them reasons to wonder?"

His hands latched on to her hips, and goose bumps pebbled the bare skin beneath his grazing thumbs. "Was I clear about how much I like this outfit?" he asked, enjoying her little shiver. "Never take it off."

"Never?" she asked, eyes glinting once more. "You sure about that?"

Somewhere far too near, a throat cleared.

Lincoln returned his hands to his sides and glared at his approaching brother, Finn.

"Morning," Finn said, whistling softly as he crossed the final few feet to join them.

Josi crossed her arms over her middle. "Hey, Finn."

"Jo-si," he said, dragging her name into two singsong syllables. "Lincoln. What are y'all up to?"

"We were just on our way to the farmhouse," Josi said, sounding infinitely calmer than Lincoln felt. "We heard you were coming and hoped to catch you."

Finn rubbed his chin. "That's what you were doing?"

Lincoln imagined tripping him.

"Sure were," she said. "Since you're here, I guess you can tell us everything over some coffee."

"Sounds great," his brother answered, rubbing his palms together and sliding a goofy look at Lincoln.

He turned back toward his cabin and led them inside.

Lincoln started a fresh pot of coffee while Finn and Josi took seats at the kitchen island.

"Well?" Lincoln asked, setting his hands on his hips as the little appliance chugged and grunted. "What do you know?"

Finn leaned forward. "For starters, you were right when you suggested the drivers from last night still trained together. I made a few calls and confirmed they're all regulars at the Barbell Club. Same place the fight-club members all trained before."

Josi released a soft breath, and the color drained from her face. She'd lost her first love to that fight club.

Lincoln straightened, wishing he could comfort her. "You think the club is up and running again?"

Tara had already lost a brother to the group, and now she was missing. This couldn't be a coincidence.

Finn rolled his shoulders, clearly as tense as Lincoln suddenly felt. "Some folks are saying yes," he admitted, "but nothing's been confirmed. I'm working on that."

Lincoln poured three mugs of coffee and passed one to Josi, another to his brother. He raised the third to his lips.

Silence reigned as he sipped.

Eventually Josi spoke. "Marcus hated fighting," she said, voice soft and eyes unfocused. "He was a good fighter, because he'd had to be. His life was never easy. At first, I thought boxing was good for him, as some kind of release. The money didn't hurt. After a while, I realized he wasn't telling me the whole story, and the amount of money he won couldn't have been a result of anything on the up-and-up. One night he told me he was quitting, because he was hurting people. I didn't understand what that meant until all the news coverage following his death."

The fights had been brutal, and they didn't end until someone couldn't leave the ring under their own power. Most were unconscious.

"He had so much anger and pain." Josi pressed a fist to her heart. "He should've gotten help to manage the emotions. Instead, he put all his energy into protecting Tara. He was determined to shield her from everything bad in the world. On the surface, he seemed to be managing. As it turned out, he was not."

"How did he and Tara end up in the system?" Lincoln asked.

Josi pressed her lips into a tight line. "Their parents overdosed together. Marcus found them one morning when he woke for school. He was eight. Tara was four."

Lincoln set aside his mug, devastated for the entire family.

"They were placed in the same foster home until she was a freshman in high school, and Marcus aged out. He worked all sorts of jobs starting when he was fifteen. Once he was a legal adult, he petitioned the court for guardianship of

Tara. Things got harder from there, because he couldn't make any real money with no formal training and only a high-school education. Then he found the fight club. Tara's grades were good, and he said he wanted her to have the future he didn't."

Josi's eyes glistened with unshed tears. "I guess he got that. At least she lived."

Lincoln set his hand on hers and squeezed gently.

Marcus had died in the ring. A blow to his head had sent him down, never to get up again. It hadn't been his first head injury that week, and according to the coroner, any physician would've forbidden him from fighting until he'd healed. But people who rely on money from an illegal fight club to make ends meet don't see physicians or take their advice.

The organization had been referred to in news articles as a bare-knuckle fight club, but according to attendees, participants weren't limited to punching. Every hit was legal, and every match was winner takes all. The amounts of money changing hands during any given fight were astronomical. The locations had changed frequently to stay off local law enforcement's radar, but eventually every secret comes to light.

"I'm sorry no one was able to help them," Finn said. "And I hate that the police weren't faster at finding and shutting down the operation."

She freed her hand from beneath Lincoln's and wiped tears from the corners of her eyes. "Let's just make sure the worst doesn't happen again."

He nodded. "I'm going to swing by Tara's place again today, talk to her neighbors, see if anyone knows where Tara might be or if they noticed a suspicious vehicle hanging around."

"We were there yesterday," Josi said. "But the kids we talked to hadn't seen her in days."

Finn's eyebrows rose. "Were you able to get inside?"

Josi frowned. "No one was home."

Lincoln met his brother's eye, understanding the question. "We didn't have reason to invade her space, so we headed over to her place of employment, then hit the bonfire."

Finn tapped his thumbs against the island's edge. "I talked to the folks at the pawnshop. Can't say anyone was very helpful."

Josi's eyes narrowed. "Did you think I'd break into Tara's place?"

Finn flipped up both palms in innocence. "No, ma'am. I trust you implicitly." His gaze drifted to Lincoln. "It's my brother who makes asking necessary."

Josi turned her focus to Lincoln. "You break into homes?"

"I can."

"You have," Finn said, tattling.

Lincoln frowned. "Only if I suspect someone is in trouble. Or when Dean and Austin are unavailable," he amended.

His brothers, Dean and Austin, ran a local private investigation company. Both were exceptional picklocks, but they were often busy. And Lincoln was better.

"Finn, cover your ears," Josi said, her wide blue eyes fixed on Lincoln. "This is weird, but I might have a key. Marcus gave one to me when we were together. I haven't thought about it in ages. I put all his things in a memory box after our split. Assuming Tara hasn't changed the locks, we might not have to break in if we want inside. If she's there, I'm sure she'll understand, and if she's not, I think she'll be glad when we find her."

"That's still illegal," Finn said, hands placed loosely over his ears. "You need permission to use the key."

"I asked you not to listen, and now you're eavesdropping," Josi said, sliding off the stool and onto her feet. "I'm going to run home and get—" Her gaze slid to Finn, then back to Lincoln. "My library books. They're all overdue. Give me a ride into town so I can return them?"

Lincoln nodded. "Yep."

She opened the door and stepped outside. "Be right back."

Finn pointed at her retreating back. "What you're planning is called breaking and entering," he called.

"You're still eavesdropping," she repeated, pulling the door shut behind her.

Lincoln laughed, and Finn spun on him. "Did you just laugh?"

"No."

"I want to make a joke about petty crime lightening your mood, but I'm more concerned with your plan to commit a Class H felony. You aren't Bonnie and Clyde, and I'm legally obligated to stop you."

"You can always come with us," Lincoln said.

Finn pushed onto his feet. "Is that before or after you visit the library?"

"Probably before."

Chapter Eleven

Josi climbed the front porch steps to Tara's home, key in hand. She sent up prayers the locks hadn't been changed, and that maybe, Tara was hiding inside.

Behind her, Lincoln and Finn argued quietly over whether or not they should be there. Finn didn't approve of the outing but saw the validity in it, and he hadn't believed her library-book story, so he'd followed them to Tara's house.

The street was eerily silent, with all the children at school and parents presumably at work.

She froze in midstep a moment later. The front door was ajar. "Guys."

The bickering stopped, and the Beaumonts instantly bookended her, attention fixed on the problem.

Finn motioned for them to stand aside, then he toed the door open with his boot, one hand on his holstered sidearm. "Marshal's Bluff police," he called. "Anyone home?"

When no one answered, he moved into the living room.

Lincoln caught Josi by the wrist when she tried to follow. "Wait."

She fought the urge to pull away. Tara was missing. She'd been shot at, and Josi had left her. The weight of that hit hard against her chest. "What if she's here, but doesn't answer because she's terrified, or because she physically can't?" What if the gunman had hit her that night, and she'd come home to heal? Then hadn't survived.

Lincoln released her, then moved into her path, a gentle expression on his usually furrowed brow. "From everything you told me last night, Tara's resourceful and her brother taught her well. We have to assume the best until we hear otherwise."

Finn strode back through the living room, then climbed the steps to the second floor.

Josi peered through the open door, fighting emotion and nostalgia at the chaotic scene before her. Everything from framed photos to the hand-me-down couch had been overturned since her previous visit with Lincoln. She hadn't been inside the home in a long while, but before that, she'd spent nearly every night with Marcus. Until he'd begun pushing her away. Even then, she'd blamed the fight club. Even before she'd known the whole ugly truth about the illegal matches and gambling. She'd grown close to Tara during the relationship's decline, both worried about a man they saw slipping away. Eventually, Josi had let him go. She'd stopped visiting Tara, and she'd started focusing on herself. Then Tara had called to say he'd died.

Now both Marcus and Tara were gone, and someone had destroyed their home.

Finn returned, tucking his cell phone into his pocket. "Come on in," he said. "Shut the door behind you."

Lincoln checked the street before locking up when they stepped inside. "No sign of a tail this time."

"Probably because they've already been inside and taken whatever they were looking for," Finn said. "Unless this mess was meant to send a message. Either way, crime-scene personnel are on the way to photograph and fingerprint the place."

Under Siege

"Tara?" Josi asked, though the answer was obvious.

Finn shook his head.

Josi turned in a small circle, examining the destruction. "Do you think they found what they came for?"

"Let's hope not," Finn said. "Here." He pulled sets of blue plastic gloves from his pockets and passed one pair to Josi and another to Lincoln. "Put these on and don't touch anything."

"Why would I put them on if I don't plan to touch anything?" Lincoln asked.

Josi made her way into the kitchen, ignoring the sibling banter. A photo of Marcus with his arm around her was taped to the refrigerator. Tara had taken the shot of them outside the Barbell Club, where he used to train. Strange that she'd kept it on the fridge.

Tara had told Josi in the days following her brother's funeral that something had broken in him. He'd become detached. Emotionally withdrawn from his life. And she hated that she'd never know what had gone wrong.

Maybe she'd finally gotten an answer, and it had cost her.

"Someone was looking for something other than Tara," Finn said. "If she knew the fight club was up and running again, for example, and she wanted to bring it down, there would be a lot of money at stake."

"When they couldn't catch her," Lincoln added, piggy-backing on the thought, "they might've come looking for whatever she had on them, maybe some kind of evidence, instead."

Josi blinked back tears as she looked into the smiling faces of her past self and Marcus. They could've had a great future, if only he'd opened up to her and been honest about what was going on. They should've been able to get through anything by leaning on one another, but he'd pulled away instead. Always determined to handle everything himself. She'd loved him, but deserved a true partner, and her heart had shredded when she let him go.

She turned away from the photo with resolve. "How can I help?"

Finn cast a weary look around the space. "Let me know if you see a laptop or cell phone. Those are most likely to have traces of where she's been and who she's been in contact with recently."

Josi highly doubted that. If Tara had a secret, she'd have hidden it better than on her phone or laptop, the first place anyone would look. She climbed onto a chair instead and checked the panels of the drop ceiling near the back door. From there, she looked behind framed art on the walls and tugged grates away from vents. Then she dug into boxes of cereal, removing the bags and contents to search the space beneath.

Lincoln and Finn stopped what they were doing in favor of watching her work.

Finn approached curiously as she dropped to check the space underneath the kitchen sink. "What are you doing?" he asked, squatting beside her as she ran her hand along the backside of the pipes.

"Sometimes when you grow up in foster care, or spend too many nights at a halfway house or shelter, you learn to hide your things of value. Otherwise they turn up missing."

He stretched onto his feet and moved away. "Guess we'd better look a little more carefully."

Lincoln followed him into the next room.

By the time the crime-scene team arrived, Josi had unearthed four hundred dollars in cash, an old baggie of weed, photos of Tara and Marcus taken throughout their child-

hood and a journal containing a series of entries she'd written to him since his death.

She put the journal back where she'd found it and moved
on. The words were private, the pages stained with tears. Her
heart broke anew for her friend's grief as she walked away.

One last trip through the kitchen drew her eyes to something she hadn't checked. A little red teapot on the stove.
She removed the lid and peered inside. Nothing. Then she
noticed the small key taped inside its lid.

Chapter Twelve

Later that morning, Josi curled her feet beneath her on Lincoln's couch. Finn had taken the key from Tara's teapot, and Lincoln had brought Josi home. Now, they just needed to figure out what the key unlocked.

Josi hovered a pen above a pad of blue-lined paper. She'd already scribbled several words down the center. "So far we have safety deposit box, post-office box, security box and secret lair." She groaned in frustration. So much for brainstorming ideas about the key's purpose. She moved the pen and paper to the coffee table and pulled a pillow onto her lap. "We've been at this almost an hour and all we've come up with are three basic and obvious ideas, which your brother has surely already thought of, and one desperate attempt to lengthen the list."

Lincoln's cheek ticked up. "You'll only think it's silly until we find the secret lair."

Josi tossed her pillow at him. "Stop making me laugh. I feel terrible every time I do. I shouldn't be allowed to be happy again until I know Tara's safe." It was the least she could do for Marcus. She hadn't been able to save him.

As if reading her change in mood, a mass of clouds raced over the sun outside the window, stealing the light. A distant jolt of thunder rumbled for emphasis.

"Hungry?" Lincoln asked, rising and turning for his kitchen.

"Not really." She'd been too consumed with the mystery of the hidden key to think of much else.

Behind her, Lincoln opened and closed the refrigerator and cupboards, clinking and clanging softly while she stared at her discarded, pitiful list.

It was barely lunchtime, but she was already tired. Emotionally drained and looking through the window at a world too dark for midday. The constant threat of rain since dawn seemed a perfect analogy of her life. She didn't want or need the gloomy reminder.

"It must've been hard to spend time at Tara's today," Lincoln said. "Even harder to consider the possibility the fight club is back and connected to her disappearance."

Josi released a slow, steadying breath, because he wasn't wrong.

"How are you doing?" he asked.

She twisted on the cushion to watch as he worked, his back to her, face hidden. "I don't know. Okay, I guess. Better than Tara."

The scent of chocolate rose into the air, and she turned to watch Lincoln stirring a steamy mug. Next, he shook a can of whipped topping and created a stout cone atop the drink.

"What is that?" she asked, sitting taller as he ferried the drink to her hands.

"This makes everything better," he said. "This and food."

She accepted the drink with an appreciative smile and sipped gently, her nose dipping into the whipped topping. "I can't believe I'm saying this, but you might be becoming your mama."

Lincoln swiped the pad of his thumb across her nose, removing the dot of cream. "That's quite a compliment."

He returned to the kitchen, then back to her a moment later, two bowls of chunked fruit in hand. He set the bowls on the coffee table and settled a pair of forks and napkins beside them. His final trip came with a tray of sandwich halves. "I only had ham and cheese," he said. "There are casseroles in the freezer, but those take a while, and I wasn't in the mood for eggs and biscuits."

Her stomach growled at the sight of the food. "Goodness. Apparently, I'm starving."

"We didn't eat breakfast," he said, taking a seat at her side.

Josi started to argue, then remembered it was true. They'd never made it to the farmhouse, and she hadn't eaten at Lincoln's place before slipping away to shower and change. She traded her hot drink for a sandwich half. When that was gone, she made short work of the fruit. "Thank you," she said, slowing to breathe.

Lincoln stilled, fork halfway to his lips. "This wasn't any trouble."

"Then thank you for paying attention," she said. "For knowing I was hungry, even when I didn't realize it."

"You've got a lot on your mind," he said, then took another bite of his meal.

"Yes, but I appreciate you. I don't say it enough. You're always keeping watch. Of the animals. The ranch. Your family. Me."

He set aside his fork and empty fruit bowl.

"I know because I pay attention too," she said.

His eyebrows rose by a fraction. "Is that right?"

She nodded. "I do. And I like the easy, companionable work routines we have, but I really enjoyed getting to know you last night. I like talking with you."

Lincoln's expression strained.

She considered changing the direction she'd been going, anything to avoid the pain of rejection. But she'd lost too many things to secrets and unspoken truths. Marcus was gone, and Tara was missing. Why did people keep so much to themselves? Why did those things end up hurting her?

"I can remember the first time I saw you," she said flatly. "I thought you were so handsome. You were still enlisted and visiting on leave. I knew I had to get over that before you came home, especially if you planned to stay in town like Finn, Dean and Austin."

Lincoln turned slightly in her direction. "Then I came home the way I did, silent and hurting. Probably a little short-tempered and rude."

She lifted and dropped one shoulder. "I just saw a guy processing some impossible pain. When you started working at the stable, I saw your dedication and compassion to absolutely everything, and I was hooked."

His lips parted, but he didn't speak, so she went on.

"I know you probably see me as the troubled teen I was when I got here, or even like a foster sibling," she said, and grimaced. "But that's never been the way I see you. I thought you should know."

Lincoln studied her, then leaned forward, forearms resting on thighs. "My family told me about you when you first arrived. Mama was thrilled to have another woman around. I could tell she wanted you to stay. I didn't think much more about it until I came home, then started working at the stable. To me, you were never the teen they'd described."

She smiled. "By then I was twenty-one."

"Not a kid," he said. "Believe me. I know. You're confident, smart and strong. You always say what you want to say. I envy that." He clasped his hands and turned soft green eyes to her, peering from beneath thick, dark lashes.

"What do you want to say now?" she asked, her heart in her throat.

"I'm sorry for your pain and loss."

His words were a bullet to her heart, and tears began to form.

"You loved him," he said, undoubtedly speaking of Marcus.

Josi wiped her eyes. "I did. As much as I could. I still had a lot of growing up to do, and I don't think either of us really understood what romantic love was. We certainly hadn't had any proper examples. Beyond a friendship and mutual attraction, we were two people living two separate lives. We spent our nights together as a way to refuel and escape. Then the sun rose, and we went our ways again. Wash. Rinse. Repeat. I couldn't have fathomed then what it meant to build a life with someone, not just running parallel."

"Sounds like you had an incredibly strong friendship," Lincoln said. "That love is just as deep and powerful as any other."

"Yeah," she agreed. "I see that now. What we shared was necessary and beautiful. Exactly what we both needed at that time. But it would never have been enough for me long-term."

Lincoln pulled tissues from a box on the side table and moved closer, delivering them to her hands.

She accepted and dried her cheeks. "I want a partner and an equal, not a savior or a big brother."

Lincoln leaned back slightly, as if her words had hurt him somehow. "You deserve to get exactly what you want."

"What do you want?" she asked, the idea coming into her mind a moment before flying from her lips. "A family of your own? Children?" She'd seen him with his nieces and nephews. They adored him, and he pretended to find them irritating, while indulging their every whim and desire. Because underneath all the frowns and silence, Lincoln was a marshmallow. Soft and sweet for the people he loved.

If only she was one of the lucky ones.

"Do you?" he asked, unapologetically turning the question around.

"Yeah," she admitted. "More than anything. And I want to watch my family grow. Attend graduations and weddings. Meet my grandkids. Maybe see them graduate and marry too. I want a home bursting at the seams from laughter and abundance as I grow old." She laughed and rolled her eyes. "Not too much to ask, right?"

"Not at all."

"Your turn," she said, nudging him.

"I want a good, honest life," he said. "One that makes a difference to people in need, and I want a family as united as the one I have now. I want to honor the legacy my folks have created. Whatever form that takes is good for me."

She nodded. He hadn't answered her question directly, but it was a great answer.

Her mind took an unexpected detour then, conjuring an image of the photo on Tara's refrigerator. Josi and Marcus outside the Barbell Club. It hadn't made any sense for Tara to display them as a couple after all this time.

Then something clicked, and she reached for Lincoln with a jolt of adrenaline. "I think I might know what the key belongs to."

Chapter Thirteen

Icy chills covered Josi's skin as she stepped into the parking lot outside the Barbell Club, Marcus's old boxing gym. She'd only visited the location a handful of times, and she'd regretted each. On the first trip, she'd been shamelessly ogled and catcalled, causing a lasting beef between one of the offenders and Marcus. She'd been propositioned in the lot on her second trip and opted to wait in her car after that. Her final visit had been with Tara when she'd gone to collect Marcus's personal things following his death.

The lot was nearly empty as she made her way toward the door with Lincoln at her side. The place would get busier as the day went on and members made their way to the gym before heading home from their various shifts. Hopefully, this would be the perfect time to speak with a manager or employees who knew Tara.

Lincoln opened the glass door, allowing Josi to enter the squat cinder block building ahead of him. A mechanical chime sounded overhead. Scents of sweat and some kind of food permeated the small, poorly lit space.

Josi never understood why anyone wanted to work out there. Every time she entered, she was immediately ready to leave.

A bulky man in shorts and a ripped tank top lifted free

weights before a wall of mirrors. He wore large headphones and barely spared her a glance.

In a boxing ring at the end of the rectangular space, a set of long-limbed individuals sparred with gloves and head-gear.

"Finn's on his way," Lincoln said, glancing at his phone before tucking it away. He'd called his brother from the road, letting him know what was on Josi's mind, but Finn hadn't answered. "He said he was in a meeting earlier. He'll be here in a few minutes."

"Good," Josi said, because nothing about this building's vibe had changed since her last visit, and her skin had already begun to crawl.

The weight lifter took notice as they moved marginally closer. He eyeballed them via their reflections in the mirror. The boxers stopped to blatantly stare.

Josi found strength in the fact Lincoln was with her and a cop was on the way. Then she squared her shoulders, accessed a recent photo of Tara she'd found on social media and moved toward the duo in the ring. "Hi," she drawled sweetly, hoping to look as fragile and foolish as they likely thought she was. She'd learned long ago to keep her cards close to her chest. Too often, weak men found strong women threatening and behaved accordingly. She didn't want any trouble.

"I'm looking for my friend. Have you seen her?" she asked, turning the image to face the boxers.

Unless a whole lot had changed in the past couple of years, it was unlikely more than a few women ever visited this place. If Tara had trained here, she was sure someone would remember. Hopefully, one of these three men.

"Nah," the taller man said. He looked to his partner, and the other man shook his head.

Josi turned toward the mirror and the weight lifter locked his reflected gaze on her.

He shook his head slowly, eyes narrowing. Either in answer to her question or in warning. Regardless, she'd accept the expression as a no.

Lincoln's hand found the small of her back, urging her against his side. He turned toward an open door marked Office and took her with him in that direction. "Let's see who's working."

A balding man with a barrel chest and round belly sat behind a cluttered desk. The remnants of a sandwich was lying on parchment paper beside a paper cup of coffee and open bag of chips. "Dammit," he complained, scrolling with his mouse, eyes fixed on the computer screen before him.

Lincoln knocked on the door frame, and the man turned an angry expression toward the sound.

"What?" he snapped. His features unfurled when he saw Josi, and his eyebrows rose as he took in the large man at her side. "Can I help you?"

"Hi," Josi said, trying and failing to place the man's face. He was vaguely familiar, but maybe it was the location that put the idea in her mind. "I'm looking for a friend. She might've trained here. Have you seen her?" She turned the phone in his direction, then took a step toward the desk.

"Can't say that I have," he said. "We don't get a lot of women. I'd remember."

"Are you the manager?" Josi asked.

"Dennis Cane," he said, wiping his hands on his pants. He stood and offered his hand to her, then did the same with Lincoln.

"You box?" Dennis asked, holding Lincoln's handshake a moment too long.

"I can," Lincoln said.

The man grinned. "That's what I like to hear. What are you, one-seventy? One-seventy-five? I could use another cruiserweight."

"I'm not looking to join a gym. Thanks anyway."

He hurried around the desk. "Care to show me what you've got? Maybe we can waive the membership fee."

"Why would you do that?" Josi asked, disbelief clear in her voice. Was Lincoln being recruited for the fight club right before her eyes?

His smile tightened as he turned briefly to her, then back to Lincoln. "I'm a big fan of the sport." He motioned them into the gym. "I'm not a bad coach either. Plus, boxing's a great workout. Keeps you fit. Women love that."

Lincoln kept one hand on Josi as they moved toward the ring. "I'm not interested," he said. "Isn't this the place that was associated with that fight club?"

The older man stopped short then turned on his heels. "Only peripherally, because the man who died trained here. We've been trying to shed that stigma ever since."

"So you didn't condone it," Josi said. "Were you here when that all went down?"

He scrutinized her then, and she wondered if he was beginning to recall the other version of her. One that wore leather and heavy makeup. One who'd been in love with the man whose death he spoke of so casually.

Did she remember him from those days too? Was that why he seemed familiar?

Dennis schooled his features. "He got involved in that fight club on his own. It had nothing to do with this place or anyone in it."

"Why do you think people went for that kind of thing?" Lincoln asked. "Why not just box here? Like them." He motioned to the men in the ring, who'd given up all pretense of exercise and stopped to watch and listen.

The older man crossed his arms. "I suppose some people have pain they can't deal with, and they'll do anything to beat it out of themselves. Most likely it's their demons that drove them there."

Lincoln rubbed a thumb across his bottom lip, feigning thought. "That's fair. I've got a few demons of my own."

"Exorcise them in the ring," Dennis suggested, working his unkempt eyebrows.

"I don't want to hurt anyone."

The front door opened, and the mechanical chime sounded on the heels of deep male voices. A set of men toting large gym bags slowed to stare.

Josi recognized the dark-haired man in front. He used to run with the same crowd as one of the drivers from last night. The one who'd been in the back of the cop car.

Instinct gripped her tightly and she laced her fingers with Lincoln's.

She'd never had a decent experience at this place, and today wasn't shaping up to be different.

"We should go," she whispered, rising onto her toes and lifting her mouth toward his ear.

He raised a hand in goodbye to the manager. "I'll think about the offer," he said, ending the discussion of a free membership and taking her advice without question.

Josi's heart beat painfully as they moved through the exit.

"What happened?" Lincoln asked, turning her to face him once they were safely outside.

"I recognized one of the guys who just walked in. He's friends with one of the drivers from last night. Marcus introduced us years ago and warned me to steer clear. After that, I'd notice him at parties, usually causing trouble and often with a busted lip or swollen eye. I never needed a reason to keep my distance. I don't know if he's wrapped up in what's happening with Tara, but we definitely don't want a confrontation."

Lincoln opened his mouth to speak, but his gaze landed on something over her shoulder and his face contorted in anger.

Josi spun in search of the problem and found it easily.

His pickup truck sat at an awkward angle, and the tires visible to them had been slashed. A knife still stuck into one wheel.

The veins in Lincoln's arms and neck protruded as he clenched his jaw and fists.

"Don't," she whispered, watching his internal debate. "Going inside and lashing out at those guys won't get us anywhere good. Stay with me, and let's call Finn again." Her voice quivered unintentionally on her final plea.

His eyes flickered to hers, then to the edge of the lot, where Finn's cruiser finally appeared.

Josi nearly sagged in relief. "Perfect timing," she said. "We don't even have to call."

Finn parked beside them and climbed out with an exhausted sigh. "Sorry I'm late."

"You're actually just in time," she said, pointing to the truck. "We were on our way out when we ran into a little trouble."

"Oof." He ran a hand through his hair, then tugged a ball cap onto his head. "I'll take the knife into evidence and call a tow truck. Anything else I should know?"

"I'd say this is the priority," Josi said. "A group of men arrived a few minutes before we walked out."

Part of her wondered whom she'd really saved by asking him not to go back inside. By the look on his face, she wasn't so sure it was Lincoln who'd have been in the most danger.

Finn turned for the building. "All right. Give me a few minutes."

Lincoln's jaw clenched and released. His hands rolled into fists at his sides.

"Hey," she began. "Look at me."

Finn tipped two fingers to the brim of his hat, then walked away.

Josi faced off with the man before her. "Do you feel a panic attack coming? Or are you just really mad?"

His gaze snapped to hers, his shallow breaths making her pulse speed up.

Panic, she realized. "Everything is okay," she said. "We're together and we're safe. Tires are easily replaced, and Finn's handling the rest."

Cautiously, she placed her hands on his stubbled cheeks and pulled his face toward hers. "Breathe."

Lincoln allowed her to pull him closer. His eyes were expressive and focused. He might've been feeling out of control, but he was still with her.

She pressed a feather-light kiss to his cheek, hoping the distraction would draw him back from the brink of an attack, if that's where he was headed.

He expelled a long breath in response. He inhaled sharply when she pressed her lips to his. "Josi." Her name was ragged on his tongue. His balled fists opened and moved to her hips.

"There you are." She kissed the tip of his nose. Then his forehead.

And the impenetrable, stoic mountain of a man grew pliable in her hands. He wrapped long arms around her and molded his body against hers.

She pressed her cheek against his chest and listened as his racing heart slowly calmed. "Welcome back."

"Thank you."

"It was my pleasure," she said, smiling against the warm fabric of his shirt. "Feel free to return the favor sometime."

His chest bounced gently when he chuckled.

Josi pulled away as the wind increased, wrangling wind-blown locks. Clinging to Lincoln was a pastime she'd never quit given the choice, so it was best she not get too comfortable.

"Jos—" he began.

"All right!" Finn called, cutting him off. He reappeared outside the gym, hands on hips. "Tow truck is on the way."

"What about the guys who flattened my tires?" Lincoln asked, turning to face his brother.

"Cameras are down," Finn said. "No one inside saw it happen."

"Three guys had just walked in," Lincoln reminded his brother. "They either saw it happen, or they did it themselves. We weren't inside more than fifteen minutes."

Finn hiked an eyebrow. "A lot can happen in fifteen minutes. Going inside before you left doesn't make those men guilty."

Josi moved to Lincoln's side and slid an arm around his back, offering him a little of her calm.

Finn raised his other eyebrow at her, and she shot him her most Lincoln-inspired glare.

Finn grinned.

"What about the key?" she asked, changing the unspoken subject.

"I checked the locker room. All the padlocks in use open with a combination. No key needed here."

Finn moved his gaze from her eyes to Lincoln's.

She wondered what he found there, or what message was exchanged.

"The good news," Finn said finally, "is that the key definitely belongs to a standard lock, like someone would use to close a locker. We're on the right path, and I was able to rule out post-office and bank-deposit boxes."

Lincoln shifted, looping his arm around her back. "Still, doesn't exactly narrow the field."

"Well," Josi said, gently chewing her lip as another idea formed. "If we think Tara's disappearance is related to the fight club, we could still be right about the gym locker. Maybe we just have the wrong gym."

Finn frowned. "Okay. Run with this a little. Why hide a key to a gym locker that isn't directly involved with the fight club, assuming we're right about that much at least."

"Maybe the key belongs to her locker, not someone else's," Lincoln said. "That guy in there is looking for boxers. What if they've added women to the roster?"

Chapter Fourteen

An hour later, Lincoln's pickup had been towed, and he was back at the ranch with Josi.

Thankfully, there were plenty of other vehicles available. Unfortunately, none compared to his vehicle.

"I'm sorry about your truck," Josi said, waving good-bye to his parents as she climbed aboard a borrowed farm truck that smelled faintly of manure.

"Not your fault." Lincoln tugged the ancient gearshift into Drive and turned them toward the main road. They didn't have a plan of action yet, but they knew Tara wasn't at the farm, so they'd decided to get back into town and go from there.

Dean and Austin had offered him one of their nicer, newer vehicles, but considering his luck the past couple of days, Lincoln couldn't bring himself to accept. At least the old farm truck would be easily replaced if someone took another shot at them.

"It's at least a little my fault," she said. "The only reason you're wrapped up in this is because you agreed to look out for me."

He slid his eyes in her direction before pulling onto the county road. "Protecting you is a given. Any decent person would do the same thing."

Her cheeks reddened slightly at his words, and she looked away, focusing on the world outside her window.

Lincoln returned his attention to the road, hating how poorly the grandpa of a truck handled and how the body rattled excessively with every bump and dip of the road.

"Are you feeling any better?" she asked, still gazing through the glass at her side.

"Yeah." He couldn't believe Josi had recognized his brewing panic in the lot outside the Barbell Club. He hadn't even realized his anger was headed in that direction until she'd confronted him. More than that, he couldn't stop thinking about the way she'd chosen to redirect his focus.

Just the memories of her soft, strategic kisses made his chest swell. And she'd told him to feel free to return the favor. Had she been serious, or teasing? Definitely flirting. Right?

And she'd kissed him with purpose the night before. Maybe not completely as part of their ruse.

He stole a glance in her direction. This morning, she'd told him she thought he was handsome when they'd first met.

Not reclusive or mean, as he'd truly been, or practically nonverbal, which was also true in the early days of his return from the military. She'd been attracted to him. Was she still? It'd seemed that way more than once in the last couple of days, but these hadn't been normal days. Emotions were high, and he and Josi had been forced into continuous close proximity. More likely, his feelings toward her had influenced his perception of her kindness.

Regardless, he reminded himself, *there are more important things at stake right now.* And his feelings could wait.

A plume of smoke rose on the horizon as they neared a local dairy farm, and Lincoln eased his foot from the pedal.

"Have you ever eaten at the Davey farm?"

She straightened, eyes searching. "No, but I see the farmhands with milkshakes from there every summer."

Lincoln made the next turn, redirecting them toward the distant barns. "There's a little building by the road with a giant smoker. They make the best pulled pork and barbecue chicken in the county. Maybe the state. I haven't stopped there in years, but I can still taste their fresh-baked corn-bread. It's better than Mama's." He shot her a pointed look. "Never tell her I said that. I will deny it to my grave."

Josi laughed. "I could eat some cornbread. And I will never turn down a milkshake. I don't care if it's barely sixty degrees today."

Lincoln chuckled. "I'm about to make you the happiest lady in town."

Twenty minutes later, they sat on an old woven blanket in the bed of the truck, with the tailgate down. Josi dunked fries in her milkshake, shivering a little with every sip, while he made short work of a pulled-pork sandwich.

Josi's expression was thoughtful as she shook the dispos-able cup. "This experience did not disappoint."

"Better than my ham-and-cheese sandwiches?" he teased.

She stilled, then smiled. "Only barely."

Lincoln looked away, fighting a grin. Around them, the sky was gray and blustery. The setting sun was sinking lower as dinnertime drew near. The fields had been har-vested, and autumn had arrived with gusto. Silhouettes of barns and farmhouses peppered the multihued horizon. Green grass. Red barns. Tiny curls of smoke rising from chimneys. "When I was growing up, kids loved to talk about how fast and far they'd go from here as soon as they had a chance. I never understood that."

"No?" she asked.

He shook his head. "I've seen a lot of this world since high school. Some places were jaw-dropping. Almost surreal. But I'm never happier than I am in this town. Sunset at the ranch is only second to sunrise at the seaside. Marshal's Bluff has both."

Josi dangled her legs over the tailgate. "Maybe we can watch the sunrise from the beach one day."

He nodded, catching and holding her gaze. "I'd like that."

She bit her lip against a smile, and he thought again of her sweet kisses.

"I've been thinking about Tara," he said, doubling down on the problem at hand.

Her expression fell. "Yeah?"

"There can't be many other boxing gyms in town. We can take her photo and stop at each. Finn's probably planning to do the same thing. Maybe we can divide and conquer."

"Tara spent a lot of time at the Y when she was younger," Josi explained, angling to face him. "We can start there."

Lincoln gathered their trash and hopped down, then offered Josi his hand. "I'll call Finn."

Josi waved him off, climbing out independently and closing the tailgate. "I'm good. Meet you in the truck."

He watched as she rounded the pickup to her door, uncertain how he'd ruined a perfectly good moment so quickly. Accepting there wasn't enough time left on earth for him to find the right answer, he let it go.

Josi BUCKLED HER safety belt and navigated to the local Y's website on her phone. She'd been pathetically thinking of kissing Lincoln again, and he'd been wondering how many boxing gyms were in Marshal's Bluff.

She really needed to pull herself together.

Lincoln climbed behind the wheel a moment later and gunned the old engine to life. "I sent a text to Finn. He said to let him know what we learn at the Y. He's still talking to businesses near the Barbell Club, hoping to catch whoever flattened my tires on camera."

Josi sighed as she scanned her phone screen. "The Y doesn't have boxing classes," she said. "Not even aerobic kickboxing, and they only hold self-defense courses quarterly. Should we still visit?"

He drummed his palms against the steering wheel. "Sounds like we should make a new plan. Let's get a list of places with boxing classes, then set a route to visit them that won't cause a lot of crisscrossing town. Some of the places might close earlier than others. Let's figure that into the course too."

Josi did another search. "Only six local gyms list boxing on their websites. One is the Barbell Club, so that leaves five. There's one within walking distance of the pawnshop. Two on opposite ends of the beach, one closer to the high-end rental properties, the other near Old Downtown. The last one is the farthest, but still in Marshal's Bluff. It's called Body by Bella."

"How far?"

She used her thumb and forefinger to enlarge the map. "Half an hour from here. Nowhere near Tara's home or work."

"Let's start there," Lincoln suggested. "On the chance she planned to infiltrate the fight club, she'd want to train out of sight. Maybe somewhere she wouldn't run in to anyone who'd report back to folks who knew Marcus."

Josi's stomach tightened. "I hate that this is even a possibility. What was she thinking?" She rested her phone in her lap and frowned at the windshield. "Never mind. If we're right about what she was up to, then we know exactly what she was thinking." She'd wanted to stop another fighter from dying at the hands of an illegal fight club. She might've even thought she could make Marcus proud. But she'd never had to try to make him love her. He'd never been anything other than proud of his little sister.

The drive to Body by Bella took more than thirty minutes, thanks to five-o'clock traffic.

Josi was thrilled to see the bright pink sign come into view.

Unlike the Barbell Club, Bella's had a full parking lot, and the pretty, two-story structure was painted white with murals of climbing greenery and blooms on the bricks.

Women came and went in handfuls, most carrying metal water flasks and toting yoga mats. A petite blonde held the door for Lincoln and offered a flirtatious wink.

He scowled, and Josi tried not to smile.

Inside, the space was light and airy with hanging plants and low, relaxing flute music that reminded Josi of a spa.

"Can I help you?" A brunette in her late thirties smiled from behind the desk.

"Hi. I'm Josi. I'm looking for my friend," Josi said, turning her phone to face the woman. "Do you recognize her?"

"I'm Bella," she said. "Let's see." She accepted Josi's phone and pulled it closer then smiled. "Oh, sure. That's Tara."

Josi's heart leaped. "That's right. You know her?"

"I do. She hasn't been around for her usual classes this week, but she's the best." Bella furrowed her brow. "You said you're looking for her? I hope everything's all right."

Emotion pricked Josi's eyes. Things were far from all

right. "When was the last time you saw her?" she asked. "How did she seem?"

Bella's frown deepened. "About four days ago, I guess. Why? What's going on?"

Lincoln tapped his phone screen, presumably relaying the discovery to Finn. Body by Bella was Tara's gym, and likely the place where she kept a locker.

"What's going on?" Bella repeated, taking notice of Lincoln and crossing her arms.

"This is my friend Lincoln Beaumont," Josi said. "He's helping me look for Tara. She's missing."

"Missing!" Bella gasped. Her gaze darted over the busy gym, then flicked back to Josi and Lincoln. "Y'all better come back here, because I'm going to need more information."

She led them behind a welcome desk, away from the waves of incoming and outgoing ladies. Then she leaned against the far wall and nodded. "Go on."

Josi took a deep breath and explained what had happened at the motel.

Bella covered her mouth. "I knew you looked familiar."

"You've seen me?" Josi asked. Hopefully not on the local-news website.

"Mmm-hmm."

Lincoln muttered something unintelligible under his breath, then stated, "We're trying to find Tara before the shooter does, so if there's anything you can share that will help us, we'd love to hear it. We're working with local law enforcement, but we keep coming up short. My brother is the detective assigned to her case. He's on his way now."

Bella blinked—she was processing that information, or was stunned silent, Josi wasn't sure. She still hadn't answered her question. How did she recognize Josi? She was sure she'd never seen Bella before.

"We found a key," Josi said, when Bella failed to speak again. "Detective Beaumont will have it with him when he gets here. We think it might be to Tara's locker, and maybe something inside will help us know what she was up to before going missing."

Bella dropped her hand away from her lips and opened a nearby slatted door. A moment later, she raised a pair of bolt cutters. "You don't have to wait for a key."

They hurried behind her to the locker room. Bella asked the handful of women inside to step out and give her a few minutes. They quickly obeyed.

She stopped at the end of a row near the showers. "I've had a feeling something was going on with her for a while, but she always smiled and blew off my concerns when I asked." Bella lifted her cutters to the padlock in question, and it fell free. She collected it from the ground before opening the door. Inside, the same photo of Josi and Marcus from Tara's refrigerator was held in place with a large magnet. "She hung this up the day she bought her membership."

So that was how she'd recognized Josi.

"How long ago?" Lincoln asked.

"About a year ago." Bella passed Josi the lock.

"This one takes a key," Josi said, turning the lock to show Lincoln.

Bella took a seat on the wooden bench outside the lockers, still visibly shaken by the news about Tara.

"What did you mean when you said something was going on with Tara lately?" Josi asked.

"At first she was hungry," Bella said. "Dedicated. Motivated. I assumed she had some anger to work out, maybe something to prove. She was a regular from the start, using the weights and frequenting the yoga studio. She never missed a self-defense or boxing class. After a while I assumed she was fine. Maybe she'd just turned over a new leaf and realized this was all a lot of fun." She motioned around the locker room. "I've always loved fitness, so it was an easy theory to get behind."

"But?" Josi asked.

Bella wet her lips and looked briefly at her sneakers. "One day she started showing up with bruises. She had excuses, but I know what it looks like when a woman is being abused. Someone was hitting her. That was obvious. So was the fact she didn't want to talk about it. I didn't push. I wanted this to be a safe space. I didn't want her to feel uncomfortable or stop coming."

Josi looked to Lincoln and he grimaced.

"We don't think it was a boyfriend who hit her," he said.

"What?" Bella asked. "Then who?"

"We're not sure," Josi hedged. "Can you tell us more about the classes she frequented?"

Bella's frown returned. "She liked the advanced self-defense courses and cardio classes, like kickboxing, but she also sparred regularly in the ring upstairs. She was getting good before the bruises began. I assumed—"

"How long ago did the bruises begin?" Lincoln asked.

"A few weeks?" she said, guessing. "I'm sorry, but I don't understand who would hit her regularly, if not an abusive romantic partner."

The locker-room door swung open, stalling Josi's response.

Finn strolled into sight a moment later, wearing a plain black hoodie and matching baseball cap.

Bella's mouth fell open.

He flashed his badge, gaze moving over the trio. "Detective Beaumont, Marshal's Bluff PD," he said, focusing on Bella.

"Bella."

His eyes fixed on the lock in Josi's hand. "May I?"

Josi passed the lock into his hand, and he slid Tara's small key easily inside. With one gentle twist, the device opened.

Chapter Fifteen

Josi made informal introductions between Finn and Bella, then let him take over from there.

Bella appeared interested in the handsome detective's attention. Unfortunately for her, and all the other single women in town, Finn was taken. More than taken, really. He was deeply in love. All the Beaumont brothers in Marshal's Bluff had met their soul mates in the last year or so, pairing up in ways that seemed like fate. The family had a way of building relationships stronger than any armory.

Josi envied them, though she was also elated for their joy.

Everyone deserved happiness, even the grouchiest, most wonderful man she knew.

Especially him.

Lincoln caught her staring, and she turned her attention to Bella and Finn once more.

"Here." Bella pulled business cards from the pocket of her yoga pants. She passed one to Josi and another to Finn. "If there's anything I can do, or that anyone here can do, let me know. Tara is beloved. Any one of my staff members or her classmates would gladly help."

Josi nodded, fighting a burst of emotion, and moved to the open locker door.

One of Marcus's hoodies hung on a metal hook inside.

A bag of toiletries and a pair of pink boxing gloves were lying on a shelf—Marcus's initials had been written in marker along the laces.

Finn moved to her side. "May I?"

She stepped back, allowing him access, and he donned a pair of blue gloves before sifting carefully through the collection of things.

He ran his hand over the shelf and removed an envelope from beneath the boxing gloves. His focus tightened as he lifted the flap and shook the contents into the opposite palm.

"Newspaper clippings?" Lincoln asked.

Josi felt her heart break. The thin stack of articles were about Marcus's death, the fight club where he'd died. She felt the air seep from her lungs. Tara had been in so much pain, and though she'd been like family to Tara at one time, Josi hadn't visited after the funeral. She'd stayed away, licking her own wounds instead.

She'd told herself she was letting Tara take the reins, and she'd gladly visit when Tara reached out. But she was hiding and healing while Tara suffered.

Lincoln set his hand on Josi's shoulder and leaned her back against his chest.

The offering was exactly what she hadn't realized she needed. She turned and hugged him, intensely thankful for his presence, his family and his big, quiet heart.

The locker-room door opened, and a bevy of females entered, sending Josi back a step.

"I've got this," Bella said, standing and moving to meet the group. "Classes are changing. I can close the locker room temporarily, but some folks still will need to come in and retrieve their things."

Finn glanced up. "I only need another minute."

Bella hurried to corral the incomers, and Finn turned back to his work.

"Bingo." He raised a cell phone from the locker, eyes flashing. "I'll get this to the lab and see what they can learn." He dropped the device into an evidence bag, then took several photos of the locker and its contents before bagging the rest of Tara's things.

Josi hugged herself, still hating the possibility Tara had willingly put herself in the same position that had gotten her brother killed. "Do you think we're right about the fight club opening again?" She needed to know. Finn was a detective. He could be logical and objective. She couldn't stop imagining the worst possible scenario.

"We're treating every lead and theory as fact until proven otherwise," he said, sidestepping her question, something the Beaumont men excelled at.

She lowered herself onto the bench where Bella had sat moments earlier. A wave of nausea hit hard. Marcus would be utterly heartbroken if he knew this was happening. He'd designed his life around Tara's protection and happiness. Not only would he be crushed by the way her grief had festered instead of healed, but that she'd also put herself in harm's way, likely because of him.

Josi leaned forward, resting her face in her hands. "This is so messed up. What was she thinking?"

"Probably about justice," Finn said flatly. "Vigilantism isn't as uncommon as you'd think, and it doesn't usually involve crime-fighting superheroes. Usually it's just regular people who are hurting and want to do something to ease their pain, or find a deeper meaning in a loved one's death. They rarely feel any better in the end, and a lot of times they wind up in jail, hurt or worse."

Lincoln smacked the back of Finn's head.

"Hey." Finn touched the spot his brother had hit. "What?"

Josi shook her head. "You might want to work on your pep talks."

Bella reappeared, hands clasped before her and perfectly sculpted eyebrows held high. "All set?"

"Yep," Finn said, closing the empty locker and collecting the evidence bags in his arms. "Thank you."

Outside the locker room, Finn followed Bella to the welcome desk while sweaty women with curious eyes hurried inside to shower and change.

Josi and Lincoln headed for the borrowed truck.

The sun had set, leaving only a faint gray-blue glow of twilight on the horizon, and long shadows cast by short buildings over the streets and town. The headlights of an approaching car caused Josi to step aside and squint.

She blinked to adjust her eyes, but the low-slung sports car stopped several feet away, trapped in an aisle where nearly every parking spot was full. Something about the ride gave Josi the creeps. The driver was obscured by darkness and the striking glint of security lights overhead.

She hurried around the back of the truck and to the passenger door, assuring herself the driver only wanted Lincoln's parking space.

Lincoln took his time, keeping watch on the car as he approached the driver's-side door.

Then the little car's passenger door opened, and a man emerged. Tall and lean in a black leather coat and knitted ski mask, he moved swiftly in Josi's direction.

"Back off," Lincoln warned, heading toward her as well.

The man's arm snaked out and caught Josi before Lincoln reached her side. He pulled her against him and dragged her back a step, pointing at Lincoln with his free hand. "Stay back."

Josi squelched a scream. The leather of his jacket was ice against her neck. His gloved hand a vise on her ribs. A whimper escaped as the men stared at one another, Lincoln moving closer with each passing second. Her assailant could be armed. He could be the gunman. Lincoln could be shot.

"Let her go," he warned, his voice cold, eyes hot. His long-limbed body moved forward in slow, predatory strides.

Josi's eyes flickered to the building. Finn was still inside. He was armed and trained. He had the authority to arrest this man and stop her abduction. She just had to get his attention. On a sharp inhale of breath, she closed her eyes and opened her mouth. Then, she screamed.

The assailant's outstretched hand snapped back, locking under her chin and pressing her mouth closed. His long, angry fingers gripped her jaw and dug against her cheekbones. "Shut up," he hissed. "You should've left this alone," he growled. His mask-covered cheek rubbed against hers. "This is your fault. Understand?"

Her eyes filled with hot tears.

"Last warning," Lincoln said, finally within striking distance.

The car's engine revved menacingly, as if it might launch forward and crush him if he took another step.

Her abductor dragged her toward the open passenger door.

Adrenaline spiked and air whooshed from her lungs. Her body jerked into motion. A hundred self-defense lessons rushed into mind, and her limbs reacted, even when her mind struggled to keep pace. She thrust up her arms, smacking the man's ears with the palms of her hands, then she curled her fingers and yanked down on his earlobes, mask and all.

He screamed and cussed, releasing her by an inch.

An inch was all she needed.

She jerked her head forward and thrust it back, connecting her skull with his face. The crunch that occurred was bone-shattering.

His hands flew to his nose, and Josi was free.

She ran for the building, screaming as she flew. "Finn!"

Behind her, the sound of landed blows and guttural roars began.

The gym door burst open, and Finn stormed out, eyes fixed on the fight occurring behind her. "Marshal's Bluff police!" he called.

Bella pulled her inside. "I'm calling the police," she said, raising a cell phone to her ear.

Together, they watched from behind a closed glass door, as Lincoln traded a series of powerful blows with her attacker. Each man was fast and ruthless. Each hit was brutal.

"Two men in a dark-colored sports car," Bella said, presumably to whomever had answered her call.

Josi's gaze swept to the waiting car.

The driver emerged and yelled for his friend.

The distraction granted Lincoln a golden opportunity. A series of one-two punches sent Josi's attacker reeling backward before landing flat on the ground.

Finn jogged to the first man's motionless form, while Lincoln turned for the driver.

The larger man's attention ping-ponged from his fallen friend, now being handcuffed, to Lincoln, then to his car, as if he might be able to get in and drive away.

Lincoln ran at the driver, landing several hits before he returned a single blow. The fight continued full force for several long seconds. Each hit to Lincoln's ribs and torso caused an ache in Josi's chest.

Then Lincoln connected a fist with the driver's chin, and he fell like a sack of potatoes.

She shoved back through the door, running for Lincoln as Finn approached the second man with handcuffs.

Lincoln rubbed his hands, flexing and stretching the digits a moment before she crashed into him. His arms came around her instantly, lifting her slightly off her feet as he squeezed. "I'm okay," he said, breaths rushing and heart pounding against her.

Finn stood and scoffed. "I can't say the same for these two. I'll have to get a pair of ambulances out here now. I can't read them their rights until they wake up." He opened his phone, clearly put out. "It's as if they didn't recognize a Beaumont when they saw one." He offered a cheesy smile to Lincoln, then stretched out his hand.

Josi held on to Lincoln as he accepted the low five. Seeing him fight had been terrifying. She'd lost her first love that way. She couldn't bear to lose her second.

Her eyes darted to Lincoln, the realization hitting like another knockout punch.

She didn't just have a crush anymore. She'd fallen in love with him.

Chapter Sixteen

The next day was slow at the ranch. Lincoln was sore and aggravated about every scrape and bruise. He hadn't lost the fights, but he hadn't gotten the best of his opponents easily either. The men had been well trained and accustomed to winning. He saw the confusion in their eyes when Lincoln held his own. But Josi had been in danger, and that knowledge alone would've kept him on his feet and swinging for as long as it took.

No one would ever hurt her on his watch, and that would be true for as long as he had breath in his body, whether she felt the same for him or not. He'd never stop protecting her.

They'd spent the night at his place again. She'd taken the bed this time, and he'd insisted on the couch. Unlike the night he'd spent with her in his arms, he hadn't slept. Every movement and deep inhalation brought the painful reminders of his parking-lot brawls.

Now, they headed home from breakfast at the farmhouse, covered plates of leftovers in hand. As if they could possibly still be hungry. And Josi watched him as if he might break.

"Do you want me to carry one of those?" she asked, eyes wide and expression eager.

"I've got them," he said, moving his attention back to his

cabin, which they were approaching. His hands screamed from effort, though the burden they carried was light. He hadn't fought without gloves in a long while, and he'd forgotten how much the pain of impact could linger in his wrists and bones.

"I wish she wouldn't send so much," Josi said. "I feel guilty when I have to throw any of it away."

He knew the feeling. His mother fed everyone with determination, one of her many ways of showing love. She'd made all their favorite dishes for breakfast, and his brothers had shown up, knowing full well what would be served. Mama was nothing if not consistent, and when someone was hurt, physically, emotionally or otherwise, she hurt too. And she did everything she could to ease that person's pain. Beginning with food.

Josi stopped in the grass between cabins. "Your place or mine?"

"Mine," he said, continuing to the door. As far as he could tell, she rarely invited anyone inside her home, and he wasn't about to invite himself.

They shed their coats and boots in the small entryway, then settled onto the couch.

She turned on the television, then navigated to the local news. "I'd hoped Finn would have more to tell us at breakfast," she said, returning the remote control to the coffee table and curling her feet beneath her on the cushion. "I hope he'll call later with an update."

"He's got four men in jail now," Lincoln said. "That's something. Two from the car chase and two from last night. I'm sure the cops are pressing them for information and using them against one another however they can. Eventually, a weak link will emerge."

"I hope so," she said, resting back against the cushions.

"If they keep underestimating you, Finn will have the whole crew off the streets soon. I guess that's one way to eliminate the problem." She rolled her head to face him. "How are you doing?"

He stiffened at the reminder she thought he was delicate. "I'm fine."

"You should've let the medic check you out last night," she said. "Or at least have gone to your family physician today."

"I'm fine," he repeated, a little more roughly. He'd grown up a Beaumont. He'd spent years in the military. He knew his way around minor injuries. Neither opponent had managed to hit his face or head, and his torso was tough. He suspected a bruised rib or two, but there wasn't anything that could be done about that. And his hands were wrecked, but nothing was fractured or broken, so they too would heal with time.

"Stop saying that," she ordered. "Look at you." She reached for his hands and cradled them in hers, turning them gently for a full review. The differences were vivid and grand.

He could probably circle both of her small wrists with one thumb and forefinger. The imagery stopped him midbreath.

"Did I hurt you?" she asked, stilling her soft hands on his calloused palms.

"No." The answer was too husky, a ridiculous giveaway, and her eyes flickered to his.

He hated the dance they'd been doing. But the voice inside him insisted this wasn't the time for such discussions. Her friend was missing. Her life was in danger. Romance, or the possibility of anything like it, had to wait.

She returned to examining the bruises and scrapes on his knuckles, trailing her fingertips lightly along his skin.

"Is it awful that I've enjoyed the last couple of days?" she asked quietly. "Not the reason things have been the way they are, but the parts where you and I are getting to know one another."

He followed the path of her fingers with his gaze, transfixed by their motion and the resulting rise in his pulse. "No."

"Good, because working with you taught me a little about who you are. This has been something so much better." She met his eyes briefly, then looked away.

"Taught you what?"

"Big-picture things," she said. "Like your compassion, diligence and general disposition. Talking to you the last couple of days has let me know you, and I like it. So I'm struggling to regret what's happening, because without the trouble, we might never have been more than a stable manager and a ranch hand."

Lincoln swallowed hard and pulled his hands away, rubbing them against his jeans.

She let her hands fall onto her lap. "See? Awful."

He shook his head and smiled at her pretty face. "I hope you plan to keep my secrets. You talked me out of a lot of information the other night. Some of that stuff, I've only told my brothers."

Josi's eyes widened, and he rewound his words.

"What did I say?"

"When we were at Tara's with Finn, I found a journal she'd been writing in," Josi said. "She was writing to Marcus, so I only skimmed the first entry. I put it back and didn't mention it, but maybe I should have."

Lincoln waited, unsure where she was going with this. "She told her brother everything too?" he asked, linking her new train of thought to his words.

"Not everything—not before he died anyway. But maybe now." She pressed her lips together. "What if she wrote about the fight club, or whatever she'd gotten involved in before she disappeared. The journal might help us find her, and it could help Finn figure out where the club meets."

Lincoln leaned away, reaching for his phone on the coffee table. "I'll give Finn a call, but I think we should wait for him before we go." The place was a crime scene now, and people were coming out of the woodwork to stop their personal investigation.

"Okay," she agreed.

Lincoln passed on the theory to his brother, and Finn agreed to meet them at Tara's place in two hours.

"Two hours?" She deflated and tipped over, resting her head on the arm of the couch. "What are we supposed to do now?"

"How about a walk?" he suggested, rising and looming over her, one hand outstretched.

She accepted, allowing him to pull her onto her feet.

JOSI SOUGHT LANCELOT the moment she entered the stables. She hadn't spent much time with the stallion lately, and she missed their quiet moments. She was sure he felt the same.

Lincoln trailed her, leaving space between them as he checked on the other horses and moved things into their proper places. It was nice that the ranch had enough staff members to cover their jobs while they focused on Tara, but there was also plenty to be said for the system Lincoln and Josi had perfected months ago.

Eventually, they moved to a stack of piled hay bales outside the far door. The sky was clear and blue with no sign of rain. It would be the first time in several days. Maybe that was a good omen.

She climbed to the top and rested her back against the barn, her boots resting on the bale below. Lincoln smiled up at her then followed. Jangling wind chimes on the farmhouse and clucking chickens in the field played the afternoon score.

"Penny for your thoughts," Lincoln said, sitting close enough to her that their shoulders touched.

"I was thinking about how lucky I was to find this place. That your parents saw something worthy and redeemable in me. And that I wasn't so damaged that I pushed them away." Because there had been a time in her life when she wouldn't have accepted their offer, unwilling to believe there was anything good in her future. But when she'd met the Beaumonts, she'd dared to hope for something more. "I feel guilty sometimes, when I see other people struggling. I wonder why I was so lucky."

"I've spent a lot of time thinking something similar," Lincoln offered, surprising her to her core.

She hadn't asked. But he'd offered. And she wondered if that was because she'd told him how much she liked getting to know him. Until the last few days, she'd rarely asked anything of him. He was so quiet, she didn't want to push or disturb his peace. Now that he'd volunteered the information, she couldn't help wondering if he wanted her to know him too. "Really?" she asked, testing the theory and encouraging him to say more.

"Sure," he said. "I think everyone asks themselves that at one time or another. Why do some people coast through life while others can't catch a break? Why do some folks have the worst parents possible, but others are handed everything they need for success? There's no logic or reason to it."

"Exactly." She leaned against his shoulder, impressed

but not surprised to discover one more way she and Lincoln saw the world similarly. "What do you think the answer is?"

He sat taller, angling to look at her. "I spent weeks thinking about all this when I was captive. The best thing I could figure is that things come to us all the time, good and bad. And we have to make choices. Every day we make a thousand choices. What to eat or wear. What route to take. Who to talk to. Whether we accept or reject what's right in front of us. If we're going to settle or fight."

"I like that," she said.

"Me too. Probably because it puts the power in my hands and leaves it up to me if I succeed or fail," he said. "I've never been one to accept helplessness, but this theory works for people who fear decision making too. Inaction still leads to a result. Inaction is a choice."

Something changed in his expression, and goose bumps skittered down her spine.

"Penny for your thoughts," she said, whispering his words back to him.

His expression hardened, and his frown became something more like resolve. He raised a tentative hand to her jaw and curved one long finger beneath her chin. His moss-green eyes locked with hers and the thrill of anticipation shot through her. "The other night, when I kissed you at the party, it wasn't just for show. I've wanted to do that for a long while."

Josi bit her lip against a smile, heart soaring. "Oh, yeah?"

His gaze fell to her mouth. "I'd really like to do it again."

She angled her mouth to his, and the delicious pressure was even better than she recalled. The best part was knowing he wanted her too.

Lincoln pulled back too soon, resting his palm against

the side of her neck and sliding his fingers into her hair. He searched her face, presumably gauging her reaction.

Josi relaxed into his touch. "Do you know how long I've been waiting for you to kiss me like that?" she asked softly, breathless. If he knew, he'd probably think she was a stalker.

The surprising glint of pleasure in his eyes was enough to melt her on the spot.

The kiss that followed was hot enough to send the whole world up in flames.

Lincoln cradled her body as he explored her neck and mouth, gliding his tongue over hers in a slow, erotic rhythm that made her see stars. There was care in his touch and reverence in his gaze when he finally pressed his forehead to hers. A light swear escaped his lips, an exclamation of pleasure.

Somewhere deep inside her, the pieces of her long-broken heart knit themselves back together.

"That was—" she began, faltering quickly at a complete loss of words. And dizzy from the sheer perfection.

"Everything," he offered, finishing the sentiment for her. "Absolutely everything."

Chapter Seventeen

Lincoln's ringing phone stopped him from kissing Josi again. Before he could curse his brother's consistently terrible timing, a trio of farmhands moved into view a dozen yards away.

Josi laughed quietly as she smoothed her hair.

"Hello, brother," Lincoln said, answering the call.

"New plan," Finn said. "I'm headed to the ranch. Will you and Josi be around?"

Lincoln initiated the speaker option and leveled the phone between them. "She's with me now. I thought we were meeting at Tara's place."

Josi frowned. "What's going on?"

"Give me about an hour. I'd rather talk with you in person. See you in a bit." He disconnected and left them hanging.

"I hate when you guys do that," Josi murmured. "Y'all are the worst at answering questions."

The farmhands reached the stable, Community Days banners draped over crooked arms. The event would be back again soon, and the ranch would be filled with visitors. Not something Lincoln could bring himself to worry about at the moment.

The men tipped their hats in greeting before moving inside.

Lincoln cleared his throat, suddenly torn. Had they seen him kissing Josi?

Would news get back to his family before he could tell them himself?

What would he say?

Josi stood, knocking hay from her backside. "I guess we'd better head home and wait."

He followed her across the field at a respectable distance, hands deep in his pockets to stop himself from reaching for her.

Inside his cabin, he poured a mug of coffee and leaned against the sink, unable to think of anything other than their kisses. Josi felt exactly right in his arms. The moment had been tender, but the experience was powerful. He was certain there were parts of him that would never recover, yet he'd sacrifice them all for another kiss like that.

"Why are you in your head right now?" Josi asked, moving into the kitchen.

He cringed internally, recalling all the reasons he'd previously told himself not to act on his feelings for her. She was five years younger. Her friend was missing. Her emotions were high. His parents and brothers saw her as family.

"Coffee?" He lifted his cup with the question.

She rolled her eyes and moved in close, long hair falling over her shoulders as she relieved him of his cup. "Always dodging my questions."

He smiled as she sipped. Apparently, today's kiss had broken some unspoken boundary. He was sure she wouldn't have taken his cup before, or stood so incredibly close. The new familiarity was delicious and intoxicating. Sharing space, coffee and secrets with Josi, while handling whatever came their way, was all he needed for a happy life.

She set aside the mug and studied his expression. "Do you regret kissing me?"

"Of course not." He furrowed his brow deeply in offense. Had he said or done something to suggest as much? "Why would you ask me that?"

"Are you sure? I'm a lot younger than you, you know."

Lincoln caught the flash of mischief in her eyes and relaxed. "I'm well aware."

She slid a palm up his chest. "I'm also your boss, which is incredibly awkward."

"Maybe we should talk to HR."

She stretched onto her tiptoes and curved her arms behind his neck, pressing her body to his in a long, heartwarming embrace. "I hope they figure it out, because I really enjoyed the kissing."

A laugh broke on Lincoln's tongue, and his lips parted in an all-teeth smile. He felt silly and young. Unlike anything he'd felt in far too long.

"I know Finn's on the way," Josi said, "but I wonder if there's time for a little more..." She kissed his jaw lightly then caught his earlobe in her teeth.

Lincoln scooped her off her feet before she'd finished speaking, making her scream with delight. He set her on the counter, heat flashing in his eyes.

"So you aren't going to make me beg," she clarified, chin tipped up at him, clearly pleased.

He stepped into the space between her parted thighs. "Do I look like a fool?" he asked, dropping his mouth to her lips. "Darling, you will never have to ask me twice for affection."

She tangled her fingers in his hair and locked her ankles around his waist. The move drew a needy moan from both of them.

Lincoln kissed her deeply and slid his hands beneath the hem of her shirt. His long fingers grazed her flat stomach, then moved up the length of her sides. When the pads of his thumbs found firm, peaked nipples beneath the thin fabric of her silky bra, he growled into her open mouth.

Josi devoured the sound, meeting his tongue stroke for stroke as she explored the skin beneath his shirt as well. Intensity climbed as they moved together, hot and greedy. When her hands reached the button on his uncomfortably tight jeans, he stepped back with a hiss of breath.

He caught her gaze and held it. "We don't have to rush," he said, the words coming in short pants. "We have all the time we want."

She removed her shirt in response.

Breath whooshed from him as he gripped her sides, taking in the sheer beauty before him.

Josi raised an eyebrow in challenge.

He pushed away the material of her bra, exposing one perfect breast, and her back arched in response. Gooseflesh pebbled her skin.

"So damn beautiful," he whispered, lowering his mouth to hers. He kissed her slowly, teasing her hard nipple with his thumb until she whimpered.

Then he lowered his head to press wet kisses against her curves.

She gasped as he closed his mouth over the tight peach bud, suckling until she called his name.

Her hands gripped the counter, one on each side of her hips, bracing herself as he lavished her with affection, affirmations and generous, heated flicks of his tongue.

Soon, her heels dug against him, pressing his jeans into the heat of her core. "More."

Lincoln's hands were beneath her, gripping her backside and hauling her off the counter. He could have her in his bed, undressed and fully sated in minutes, all without removing a stitch of his clothing. He was sure of it, and completely up for the challenge.

When they reached the darkness of his hallway, she dragged her tongue along the column of his neck to his ear. "Take me."

His doorbell rang.

His head fell forward, and he started to put her down, but she clung tighter.

She drew his mouth back to hers and kissed him slowly.

He pressed her back to the wall and willed whoever was on his porch to go away.

The bell rang again.

She allowed him to set her down. Hair mussed and lips swollen from his kiss, she ran a fingertip between nearly exposed breasts. "My shirt is in your kitchen. Can I borrow one of yours?"

He pinched the bridge of his nose, commanding his body to calm down. Picturing her in his shirt didn't help. "Take whatever you want."

"Be right back," she said, then hurried into his room without him.

Lincoln adjusted his pants and forced himself not to follow her. Instead, he turned, grabbed her shirt from the kitchen floor and tucked it into a cabinet, then went to answer the door.

Finn frowned the moment the barrier was opened. "What's wrong with your face?"

Lincoln strode into the kitchen. He needed ice water. To bathe in. "Come in."

"Are you…smiling?" Finn asked, following along on Lincoln's heels.

"No."

Finn collapsed onto the couch. He crossed his legs and set his chin in his hands, looking exactly like their mama preparing for some gossip. "Tell me everything."

Lincoln's accidental grin grew. "Stop."

"Is this about—" He pointed down the hallway, then mouthed the word *Josi.*

"Is that Finn I hear?" Josi asked, causing both men to turn in her direction. She emerged in one of Lincoln's button-down shirts with her leggings. She'd rolled the sleeves and pushed them up, as if she'd been wearing the shirt all day instead of for the past three minutes.

"Knew it," Finn whispered.

Lincoln gave him a warning look, and Finn tapped a finger against the detective shield on his belt. Lincoln rolled his eyes.

"What's up?" she asked, hiking her eyebrows as she reached the living room. "Do you have news?"

Lincoln forced his thoughts away from the feel of her in his arms. And the fact that he now had personal knowledge of what her skin both felt and tasted like.

"Nothing yet," Finn said, responding to her question. "I had to follow up on a case involving one of the guys staying on the ranch. While I'm here, I figured I'd stop by and check on you, maybe talk about Tara's case."

"Lincoln made coffee," she offered, moving into the kitchen and pulling a cup from the rack on the counter. "Can I pour you some?"

"That sounds good." He levered himself off the couch and took a seat at the island. He smiled and nodded in thanks when she delivered the drink. "I've decided to let the four guys I've got in custody go," he said. "They aren't talking."

Josi paled. "What?"

Finn lifted a palm. "They weren't budging, and I had to weigh the lost time against progress. Tara's still missing. If she's being held somewhere, we don't have days to wait. If this was a crime where the damage was done, I could drag my feet, take the full seventy-two hours to hold them, or just arrest them and toss them in jail to await their arraignment. I don't have that luxury."

"So you let them go?" Her lips parted, and her eyes shone with tears.

"I knew you wouldn't love this path," Finn said. "Which is why I wanted to talk to you about it in person. I know those men tried to hurt you. I know you feel they pose a threat, but I'm trying something else that will benefit us both. You'll be safe, and I'll get the information I need."

Josi swung her desperate gaze to Lincoln.

"You had them tailed when they left the station," he stated.

Finn nodded. "My men are on them. They won't cause you any harm without an intervention. I'm hoping they'll shift their focus to reporting back to whoever is in charge."

"Oh," Josi said, wrapping thin arms around her middle and looking less desperate. "I guess that makes sense. I've been imagining Tara being held somewhere, alone and afraid. Wondering if she's injured. If they give her food or water. People can only go so long without water."

Lincoln moved to her side, and Josi curled herself beneath his arm. She rested her head against him and let him hold her weight. "We'll find her."

She was tough and kept her chin up, but the search for her missing friend and the circumstances surrounding it were taking a toll.

He fought the urge to kiss her head or stroke her hair.

Anything to make sure she knew he had her back, and this situation would soon pass. Nothing lasted forever. Not the good stuff. And not the bad.

"What do we do in the meanwhile?" she asked, still trying to help however she could.

Finn stared at them, blinking and apparently speechless. His gaze roamed their postures and points of contact, then Josi's face and Lincoln's, before he eventually found his tongue. "I thought we'd go look for that journal you mentioned."

Chapter Eighteen

The ride to Tara's home was slow as anticipation built in Josi's chest. Too many things had happened in too short a time frame. Her mind struggled to keep up, to process the thoughts and catastrophes that never seemed to stop. Her sleep was wrecked and her nerves were shot—emotions were heightened and sharp. She wasn't over being grabbed in the parking lot outside Body by Bella. She'd need to see a therapist for years after that encounter.

In truth, she wasn't over any of the awful things happening all around her, and she wouldn't be anytime soon. Most of all she hated that Tara could die exactly the way Marcus had.

Finn was shaken as well. Josi could hear the frustration in his tone and see the unspoken emotion in his troubled eyes. Seeing history repeat itself was taking a toll on the young detective with a big heart.

Visiting the pawnshop and the party at Potter's field had taken her back to an unhappier time as well. Add in the car chases, gunman and near abduction, and Josi was definitely not okay. But for now, she had to keep her chin up and hold on to hope for good news to come.

Tara's phone call from the motel had set everything in motion. The madness wouldn't end until she was found, and whatever she'd gotten involved in was over. *The fastest way through a tough spot*, Josi thought, *is to keep going*.

Eventually Lincoln parked the borrowed farm truck in Tara's driveway behind Finn's pickup and climbed out.

Josi followed suit, meeting the brothers on Tara's porch.

Finn let them inside, then pocketed the key. "I straightened things up a little when the crime-scene team finished," he said. "The place was a mess, but nothing appeared to be stolen. Nothing obvious anyway. Her television, video games and anything else that could be turned around for quick cash are still here. Without Tara to tell us for sure, I'm going to assume whoever broke in was more interested in finding something than in removing anything."

"And you stopped by to clean up," Josi said, impressed and unsurprised.

The rooms were in one-hundred-percent-better shape than they had been following the break-in. He'd cleaned the mess, swept up broken things and neatly arranged books in stacks. He didn't know where everything went, but he'd made an effort.

Finn set his hands on his hips and turned at the waist, scanning the scene. "I didn't want her to come home to that mess, especially considering what she's already going through, wherever she is."

Josi nodded. Whether Tara was on the run, hiding out, or being held captive somewhere, coming home to a disaster would only make her feel worse. Emotion pricked her eyes and pinched her heart. "Your mama raised you right."

"She did," he agreed with a reluctant smile. "She's worried about tomorrow, trying to get every detail perfect for the next Community Days event. She's hoping y'all will be able to help, but doesn't want to ask, because she knows finding Tara and keeping you safe is more important. I told her we'd do what we could today so you could be there. I'll try to be present for as much of the event as possible, but I've got my hands full too."

Lincoln rubbed a hand against the back of his neck. "I saw some ranch hands with signs today. Before that, I'd forgotten."

Josi bit her lip. She'd forgotten too. She could hardly imagine returning to her role as stable manager, smiling for hundreds of curious visitors and nostalgic adults, while knowing Tara was still missing. She also couldn't imagine letting down Mrs. Beaumont. Not after all the family had done for her when she'd been in need. "I guess we'd better get to work."

The brothers nodded.

"Where did you see the journal?" Finn asked, fanning through a book from the pile.

She took a fortifying breath and headed for the little storage room behind the kitchen. "I'll get it."

Lincoln watched her go but didn't follow. He'd seemed on guard since Finn's arrival, but she supposed that made sense. The Beaumont family would have plenty of questions soon. Hopefully, no one would be upset by the possibility of her dating their son. After that kiss, there wasn't any denying it. She wanted to be with Lincoln, but his family was tight. She'd need their blessing, because she'd never do anything to create turmoil among people she so dearly loved. Even if that meant breaking her heart instead of theirs.

She retrieved the notebook and said a silent apology to Tara. Growing up the way she and Tara had, everything Josi did lately felt like an invasion. Yes, Tara was in trouble, and yes, she needed help. But asking everyone what she'd been up to, visiting her gym, entering her home repeatedly and going through her things felt creepy and invasive. A little

like being one of the bad guys. Josi had spent a lifetime protecting herself, setting firm boundaries and guarding her
personal business, only to crash into Tara's life and Godzilla-
stomp all over everything. Reading her personal thoughts
and feelings about Marcus was officially the lowest of lows.

Josi could only hope, for multiple reasons, the words on
the pages would help them find her, so the intrusion would
be justified.

"Is that it?" Lincoln asked, watching carefully from the
doorway.

Josi nodded, opening the thin cover and scanning the
sweet notes inside. Words of heartbreak, love and loss, from
Tara to Marcus. The first entry explained she'd bought the
journal with hope of working through her pain by express-
ing it. Also, she'd hoped to retain some sense of connection to her brother by speaking to him daily. For months,
the dates at the top of the page were in perfect sequence.
A new entry every day. Midway through the book, the entries became less frequent, then sporadic. Sometimes two
in a day. Other times only two in a week.

Lincoln moved closer and set a hand on Josi's shoulder.
"You okay?"

"Yeah." She took a steadying breath.

The handwriting in the latest entries was nearly illegible,
the strokes heavy and thick. A few words had been hastily
scratched out and rewritten. Others circled. Exclamation
points ended sentences of anger at his loss.

"She was agitated here," Josi said, tipping the journal
for Lincoln to see. "In the early pages, the writing is soft
and consistent. Here—" she fanned through the final dozen
pages "—the script becomes less uniform, then she just
starts making notes and phrases."

"May I?" Lincoln asked.

Before Josi could answer, the sound of a roaring engine turned her limbs to stone.

Lincoln darted from the room, headed back to where they'd started. "Stay here," he called over one shoulder, before vanishing around the corner.

Josi followed, the journal clutched to her chest. That sound couldn't have been good. Considering the fact she'd recently been followed and chased by multiple vehicles, she was sure she'd rather be with two strong Beaumonts than alone in the little room.

Finn and Lincoln stood shoulder to shoulder before the living-room window, curtains pulled aside for a better view of the street.

Beyond the glass, a black SUV raced forward, then braked suddenly, taking a reckless spin in the cul-de-sac where Josi and Lincoln had spoken to the little basketball players only days before. On the way back, the SUV slowed and the driver powered down the window.

Finn cursed, and Lincoln spun to face Josi.

"Get back," Lincoln ordered as his brother yelled, "Gun!"

The rat-a-tat of gunfire split the air, punctuated by a riot of shattering glass.

Josi dropped to her knees, then onto her chest behind the couch, a wild scream ripping from her lungs. Images of the gunman outside the motel sprang to mind. He'd shot at Tara, then at Josi. She squeezed her eyes shut and prayed the bullets missed everyone and everything that couldn't easily be replaced.

Lincoln's body covered hers in the next breath. His arms formed a cage of protection, his body shielding her own. "Finn!"

"I'm good," his brother returned. "Y'all good?"

Josi's body trembled as Lincoln eased upward in the

fresh silence, bringing her with him. Their breathing was loud. More destruction. First a break-in. Now, a drive-by shooting. She told herself not to wonder what might be next.

"Did you get the license-plate number?" Lincoln asked.

The sound of breaking glass caused Josi to scream once more.

Her gaze jumped from the previously broken window to the Molotov cocktail that had crashed onto the coffee table. Then to the fire spreading quickly onto the couch and along the area rug beneath.

Outside, the attacking vehicle tore away with another peal of tires.

All around them, Tara's home, the one she'd once shared with her brother, was going up in flames.

Finn raced outside, across the porch, gun drawn.

"No!" Josi cried, lunging to follow. She couldn't lose anyone else to this madness. "Stop!"

Around them, flames licked over the carpet and up the wall to the ceiling, creating a barrier unsafe to cross.

Lincoln caught her at the waist and towed her toward the kitchen. The living room was already dark with smoke. "We've got to go. Finn's fine. We aren't."

Josi coughed, as if on cue, her body accepting his call.

She scanned the space, heart thundering and tears stinging her eyes. Tara's belongings would soon be gone. If she survived whatever she was going through, she wouldn't have a home to return to, and all her cherished memories would be lost. "Wait." Josi planted her feet.

Lincoln tightened his grip and tugged her into the kitchen, closer to the back door, but Josi jerked free.

"Help me!" She turned to him, forcing the journal into his hands. "I can't let it all burn. Please," she begged. "We have to save what we can."

Lincoln hesitated, his cool green gaze flickering to the photo taped onto the refrigerator. He tugged it free and pushed it into his pocket.

"The framed photos," Josi said. "And the box on the bookshelf!"

He nodded, and together, they darted back toward the flames.

Heat had filled the space and smoke billowed around them. Gentle winds through the open door and broken window fed the flames.

"Lincoln!" Finn's voice rose through the crackling and whooshing around them. "What the hell are you doing?"

Josi opened her mouth to answer and inhaled a mouth full of smoke instead. Her throat and eyes burned. She strained to see and struggled to catch her breath.

"Josi!" Finn called. "Lincoln!"

She tried again to answer but couldn't find enough oxygen.

"Josi!" Lincoln's voice echoed his brother's.

She turned to look for him. He'd been only an arm's length away, just seconds before.

Her chest tightened as her senses dulled and panic rose. Which way was the door? How had she been overcome so quickly?

Something in her distant memory told her to get on the floor. The air was cleaner near the ground. She began to crawl, wheezing painfully as she moved. Her limbs felt unfamiliar and weak. The sounds of crackling flames mixed with whooshing in her ears.

Then she was flying.

LINCOLN SWEPT JOSI'S limp body from the floor and tossed her over one shoulder, holding her tightly to his chest. The collar of his T-shirt rested high on his nose and covered his mouth. The air inside Tara's rental home was toxic, filled with smoke and whatever chemicals had been inside the broken bottle. Flames had consumed the oxygen. Visibility was nearly gone.

Josi had temporarily vanished.

Thankfully, he'd developed an uncanny ability to sense her months before. There was something about her presence that spoke to him, alerted him. And it'd only taken a moment to find her on the ground. Now, they were moments from safety, but his ability to breathe was growing precarious.

He fumbled with the dead bolt on the back door, wasting precious seconds as he wrestled with the tiny knob. The smoke had followed them, growing denser with each passing heartbeat, lightening his head and muddling his thoughts.

Then suddenly, finally, they were free.

Lincoln stumbled down the back porch steps and onto the lawn. He lowered Josi to the ground several yards away from the home, then collapsed beside her.

Crisp autumn air and the mist of fresh rain cooled his skin and face as he lay beside her, panting to regain his breath. He rolled to his side and searched her for signs of life. When her chest rose and fell steadily, he flopped onto his back with relief.

"Lincoln! Josi!" Finn rushed to them, his voice wild.

Sirens wailed in the distance.

"What happened?" he asked. "Why didn't you leave when I ran outside to get a license-plate number? You scared me half to death."

Josi coughed and pulled up the hem of her T-shirt. Instead of exposing her stomach, she revealed handfuls of printed photographs and mementos. "I couldn't fit the box," she rasped. "I had to leave it. I tucked everything I could under here."

She peeled her eyes open as the coughing jag ended, then rose onto her elbows. "I couldn't let them burn."

A pair of EMTs appeared, jogging in their direction.

"Here," Finn called, waving an arm overhead.

"Burns?" the first medic asked, lowering onto his knees beside Josi.

"No," she croaked, then broke into a fresh fit of coughing.

Out front, a fire truck roared to a stop. Emergency flashers reflected off the sides of nearby homes.

Finn sidled up to Lincoln as the first EMT snapped an oxygen mask over Josi's face. "You okay?"

"Better now," Lincoln said, examining Josi's limbs for signs of injury or trauma.

The second medic stopped before the brothers, eyebrows raised in question.

They shook their heads.

"All good," Lincoln said, earning significant side-eye from Finn. His voice had been lower and rougher than expected.

The EMT didn't move. "May I?" he asked, gaze flickering to Lincoln's arm.

He followed the other man's line of sight to a singed mark on his shirtsleeve, then suddenly felt the burn of his wound beneath. "Oh. Yeah. Go ahead."

Finn made a sour face. "Your back is worse."

The EMT circled around for a look at Lincoln's back, then opened his medical bag and got to work. Apparently, Lincoln hadn't escaped completely unscathed.

"You're hurt?" Josi asked. She held the oxygen mask away from her face with one hand.

"I'm fine," he promised, then hissed long and hard as the medic poured something that felt like acid onto his back.

Her eyes glossed immediately with unshed tears. "Lincoln."

"Put your mask back on."

She narrowed her eyes in defiance, and tears fell.

Lincoln walked away from the medic. "You need the oxygen to clear your lungs," he said quietly. "Put your mask on, and I'll let the medic finish helping me."

She snapped the mask into place with a heated glare.

Finn snorted.

The medic went back to torturing Lincoln.

"So you got the license plate?" Lincoln asked, redirecting his attention from the pain.

Finn grimaced. "No. I got the make and model, but I was too late to get anything more. The tinted glass was too dark." He reached into his back pocket and removed a small notebook. "I found this inside the clock on the mantel before the shooting started. Josi gave me the idea to look a little more closely at everywhere that might be a hiding spot."

"What is it?"

Finn opened the cover and turned the first few pages before answering. "It's a calendar. Looks like Tara's work schedule at the pawnshop, the times for various classes at Body by Bella and a third set of dates and times in red. No details."

Josi pulled off her mask again. "What do you think those mean? Fight times?"

"She hid the calendar for a reason," he said. "Fight times are my guess too."

Lincoln crossed his arms, eyes narrowed, waiting for Josi

to replace her mask. Then he turned to his brother, still perusing the calendar. "When's the next date in red?"

A smile slid across Finn's smug face. "Tomorrow night. We just need to figure out where."

Chapter Nineteen

Thirty minutes later, Lincoln held Josi's hand as they followed Finn around the house toward the trucks. She was going to be okay, thanks to a lot of oxygen and an IV. He was still fuming that she'd been in danger yet again, and he wasn't thrilled with the EMT who'd tormented him while treating his burns.

Josi gave his fingers a reassuring squeeze as they walked.

The medics had instructed them to go home, rest and stay hydrated. A solid plan. Apparently, the only safe place for Josi these days was Beaumont Ranch.

Finn stopped to speak with a group of fire officials standing in the street, arms crossed, appraising Tara's home. He'd placed Tara's keepsakes and mementos into large evidence bags and given them to another officer on the case.

Josi hadn't released the items easily, but Finn promised to return everything to Tara as soon as possible, and she'd taken him at his word.

The home came fully into view as they reached the driveway. The fire was out. The front door stood open, the window gone. Charred, tattered curtains hung askew and blew gently from the wind.

Josi stopped short of the borrowed farm truck and turned

her eyes to Lincoln. "I didn't even think about the fact you parked in the driveway."

His attention moved to the pickup, now riddled with bullet holes.

Finn grimaced from several yards away. "At least it wasn't your ride this time," he said. "You only needed new tires. This truck is toast."

Josi leaned against Lincoln and set a palm on his chest. "The important thing," she whispered, "is that we're all okay."

Lincoln focused on her words as his heart rate began to rise. He'd run from a house on fire and been calm. He'd watched her slack face while waiting for her eyes to open, and he'd remained calm. Now, a few bullet holes in an old truck caused the panic to build?

"Hey." She patted his shirt and rose onto her toes. "Look at me." Her hand slid up to cup his jaw and pull it down to her. "Remember when I was on your kitchen countertop earlier?"

His gaze bounced to hers, meeting those teasing blue eyes. The imagery she'd provided sent his energies in a whole new direction, a much nicer reason for his elevated pulse.

"Lincoln," she whispered. "Do you remember?"

He nodded, hands moving to her waist on autopilot.

"Take me home and do it again?" she asked.

"Need a ride?" Finn called, moving toward his truck, wholly unaware of Josi's mind-boggling, life-affirming request.

She laughed softly as she tugged him toward the other vehicle. "Finn can drop us off and take care of the farm truck. We'll go home and take care of each other." She winked, and he felt a smile form on his lips.

HE'D SURVIVED AGAIN with Josi at his side, and she'd stopped his panic as it had begun to swell. She'd asked him to take her home and reminded him of the ways he'd touched her. The memory was intoxicating, but instead of kissing her senseless when he imagined her in his kitchen once more, the fantasy version of himself lowered to one knee.

He pushed away the thought. They weren't even dating. How could he think of a proposal? Maybe he'd suffered a head injury along with the burns.

A short while later, the trio boarded Finn's ride after the farm truck was dragged away. Finn started the engine and waited while Josi and Lincoln buckled their safety belts. "The fire officials say they got here in time to save the structure. Homeowner's insurance will repair the damage, and renter's insurance should replace most of the lost possessions. You were a good friend to get Tara's keepsakes out safely. I just wish you hadn't risked your own life to do it."

Lincoln examined the crowd of civilian onlookers as they rolled away. Was one of them involved in the drive-by shooting or fire? Did they see or know something that would help Finn find the culprit or Tara?

"All right," Finn said, slowing at the next intersection. "It's off topic, and none of my business, but I've got to ask. What are y'all doing?" He glanced at Josi's fingers laced with Lincoln's on his thigh. "When did that start? And does Mama know or can I tell her? Because I'm always keeping secrets for this family, and when the facts come out, which they always do, I lose points for subterfuge."

Josi snorted.

Lincoln grinned.

"Well?" he persisted. "I'm starting to lose faith in my detective skills on this case. I could use a win. Give me something." His phone rang, saving Lincoln from telling him to get comfortable with another loss.

He and Josi hadn't even talked about what they were doing yet. Lincoln certainly wasn't about to have that conversation with Finn.

"Beaumont," Finn answered, clearly aggrieved. "When? On my way." He disconnected the call and pressed a button on his dash, igniting a siren and likely the new flashers he'd had installed beneath the truck's grill.

"What's happening?" Josi asked, a mix of hope and terror in her tone. "Did they find Tara?"

"No. There was an incident at Body by Bella," he said. "Bella was alone when two men in masks pushed their way inside."

FINN MADE THE drive across town to Bella's in twenty minutes. A pair of cruisers were parked in the lot when they arrived.

Lincoln offered Josi his hand, then held on tight as they climbed down from Finn's truck and followed him to the gym's front door.

Bella sat behind the welcome desk, arms wrapped around her middle and dark makeup streaks below her eyes. She straightened, then deflated as Lincoln and the others walked inside.

Finn shook hands with the officers on his way to Bella.

Josi released Lincoln's hand and jogged around the desk, arms opening to wrap the other woman in a hug. "I'm so sorry this happened to you," she said. Her voice cracked with emotion, and Lincoln suspected this hit close to home for Josi, who'd recently been attacked as well.

Lincoln longed to go to her, but forced himself to stand down, allowing her the space she needed.

"Details?" Finn asked the officers quietly.

The taller man widened his stance and checked a small notepad. "The intruders used force to push their way inside when the owner, Bella, was preparing to close for the day. Two men then interrogated her at knifepoint for several minutes."

A sob escaped Bella, drawing Lincoln's attention back to the women.

Josi passed her a tissue box from the desk and patted her shoulder.

"They kept demanding information about Tara," Bella explained. "They wanted to know how well I knew her. What she'd told me about the fight club. Who else she'd told. Who I'd told. They wouldn't stop. And they didn't believe me when I said she'd never confided any of those details. If one of my regulars hadn't forgotten this was the night I close early every week and shown up for spin class, I don't know what might've happened." Tears flowed freely over Bella's cheeks, and she wiped frantically at her face with a wad of tissues. "They ran away when she walked in, and I called 911."

The criminals had asked about the fight club. So the theory Finn, Josi and Lincoln had been working with was confirmed.

Behind Lincoln, the front door opened again.

Bella stiffened as she had before, then sagged when a pair of women blew inside.

"Excuse me," one of the officers said. "The gym is closed."

The women with puffy red hair took one look at Bella and marched past. "Oh, my glory! Who did this?"

The other lady followed. "We were just leaving the café

and saw the cruisers. We had to stop. We wanted to be sure everything was okay."

Finn scratched his head and sighed. "Everything is under control. Bella's okay."

The women turned slowly to face him, comically so. Their thinly sculpted eyebrows hiked up in challenge.

"I think we'd like to hear that from her, if you don't mind, Officer," the redhead stated flatly.

"We prefer to speak for ourselves," the other added, sounding exactly like their mama.

Finn's mouth pulled low on each side, and he cut his eyes to Lincoln, who struggled not to laugh.

The woman hustled over to Bella, and Finn locked the door, then instructed one of the officers to keep it locked when the women left to avoid further interruptions.

"It's all so awful," Bella told her friends. "I can't think straight. I don't even understand what they want from Tara or why they're badgering me. Aren't they the ones who have her somewhere? And what did they mean about a fight club?"

"Tara Stone?" the redhead asked, gaze roaming from Bella to the officers.

"Do you know her?" Finn asked, stepping forward as Josi offered Bella the entire box of tissues.

"I do," the woman said. "I'm Eileen. I take self-defense classes with Tara." Her eyebrows knitted as she considered something. "She came over for pizza one night after class and asked to crash on the sofa. She said she'd had a glass of wine and didn't want to drive home, but honestly, she barely touched the wine. Or the pizza. I could tell something was off, so I let her stay, but she didn't say a word about whatever was bothering her. She ate a huge breakfast the next morning, showered and borrowed some clothes. I noticed a lot of bruising on her sides and suspected she might be in a bad relationship. Those kinds of men never leave marks where people will see. When they do, the women lie to cover for them." She shook her head, looking as heartbroken as she sounded. "You think she was involved in a fight club?"

"That's what we're trying to find out," Finn said. "Is there anything else you can tell us about that night or the following morning?"

"She made a phone call," Eileen said. "From my landline. I heard her telling someone named Petey that she was sorry. At first I thought it was the abusive boyfriend, but she told me she was supposed to be at work and needed to let him know she'd be late. That made sense."

"Petey," Josi said. "From the pawnshop." She locked gazes with Lincoln.

"Wait," the second woman said. "Did she have a bad boyfriend or not?"

Josi shook her head, redirecting her attention. "We don't think so. Why? Did she ever mention one?"

The woman bit her lip. "No, but it's curious, that's all."

"What is?" Lincoln asked, unable to stay out of things any longer. Josi looked ready to collapse, and the EMT had told her to rest. Attending another crime scene was the opposite of resting, and they needed to wrap this up so Finn could take them home.

"I saw her walking along the waterfront last week," the woman said. "I gave her a ride home. She was cradling one arm and hiding her face behind her hair. I didn't push, but I offered to help if she was in trouble. She refused everything except the ride, then she missed our class the next evening. I was terrified, but she was back in her place later that week. We never spoke about it again."

Josi frowned.

Lincoln could practically hear her thoughts. "Why would she be walking by the waterfront? She had a car, right?" He looked to Finn.

"The truck registered to her name was found near the Bayside Motel," he said.

Josi nodded. "She called me for a ride because it wouldn't start."

"I'm guessing that was more likely sabotage than an accident," Lincoln said.

Finn squared his shoulders and narrowed his eyes on Eileen. "Where was she when you picked her up? Exactly."

The woman blinked. "I don't know. It was dark. I was coming home from my girlfriend's house on Lighthouse Drive."

"That's by mile marker twelve," Lincoln said. "Which direction was she moving?"

"East," she said. "I think." The woman frowned. "Except that doesn't make any sense. There's nothing out there."

Lincoln nodded. "Sounds like a perfect place to hold a fight club."

Josi held her breath as she entered the pawnshop, steadying her nerves and shoring up her will to confront Petey. The older man had always intimidated her. Thankfully, no one intimidated the Beaumonts, and the two brothers accompanying her weren't in a mood to be trifled with.

She exhaled and squared her shoulders as she approached the counter. "Petey," she called.

The man appeared. He rounded the corner from a room beyond. "Fancy seeing you again so soon, Miss Josi." His smirk was rueful as he took her in. The expression flattened at the sight of the men she'd brought along. "What seems to be the problem, Officer?" he asked, clearly recognizing Finn.

"Detective," Finn clarified. "Last we talked, you had no idea where Tara Stone was or what she'd been up to in the days before she went missing."

Petey nodded, mouth uncharacteristically shut.

"I now have reason to believe you lied to me. Why would you do that? Interfering with an ongoing investigation is against the law."

"Hey now," Petey said, moving closer. "I was trying to protect the girl's privacy. Nothing wrong with stepping off the grid for a day or two. We all need a reset from time to time."

"A reset from what?" Josi asked, the earlier trepidation falling away like loosened binds.

Petey's gaze darted to a pair of men moving through the aisles to join him.

Josi recognized the duo from her last trip to the pawnshop with Lincoln.

Finn watched them closely, gaze shifting from the new arrivals to Petey, then back. "We believe the illegal fight club that led to Marcus Stone's death is up and running again. We also believe Tara knew about it and got involved somehow. If the man who took a shot at her outside the motel earlier this week gets his hands on her, it likely will not end well. So if you know something that can help us find her, I need that information. Now."

Josi sucked in a breath at the authority in Finn's voice. She'd never seen him in action this way. The difference between the often playful man she knew and the detective was drastic. Even at Bella's, faced with the shaken women, he'd been patient and kind. At the moment, he looked and sounded as if he might bust some heads.

Lincoln straightened at her side, and a smile tugged at her lips.

Petey and his friends were at a complete disadvantage.

He looked to the younger men, shifting and trading glances, then grunted. "All I know is she'd picked up boxing as a hobby, self-defense, all that. She told me she was paying homage to Marcus. I let it go. She missed some work from time to time, but never more than a day or two, and she worked hard when she was here." He cracked his knuckles and fixed the younger duo with a pointed stare. "If y'all know something more, you'd better talk. That girl's like a daughter to me."

They didn't respond.

"We spoke to someone who picked her up a few days before she went missing," Finn said. "According to the witness, Tara was walking alone at night near the harbor. Know anything about that?"

The shorter of the two guys, Josi remembered as Dustin, gave his friend an elbow to the ribs. "She could be in real trouble."

The taller guy ran a hand through his hair. "All right." He leaned against the nearby wall, as if he might need it for support. "T's been making money fighting other women," he said quietly. "That's all I know. Sometimes Dustin drives her to events."

"Where?" Finn asked.

"Why?" Petey said right after Finn.

Dustin shrugged, a look of shame on his crumpled features. "The location changes, but she pays me half of what she earns. I drive because sometimes she's too banged up to get home on her own. She knows that's always a possibility, so she plans ahead."

Petey scoffed. "Why'd she give you half if she was the one getting hurt?"

"I don't know, and I didn't ask. It was easy money. I need it, and she never seems to care about it. The rest was none of my business."

Josi felt her stomach pitch as details from the past rushed back to mind. "The fight referee won't call a winner until someone is physically unable to leave the ring. One fighter has to be out cold or too injured to continue." It was the only rule. Fighters had to fight until the very end.

For Marcus, it had been his life's end.

Imagining Tara choosing to climb into the ring, knowing what had happened to Marcus, was too much. Josi pushed aside the ideas as tears began to well once more. How awful must every fight have been for Tara? And she kept going back. Why would she do that?

"She didn't care about the money," Josi whispered, answering her silent question with the guy's words. "She was there to tear the place down."

Lincoln's strong arms circled her waist and turned her toward him, gathering her carefully against his chest.

Finn moved forward, tucking the two of them behind him. "Did you watch the fights?" he asked Dustin.

"Sometimes. It's not my thing. Gets too bloody. There are medics on hand, but they aren't very good. Tara always wanted to know who was taking the money and who seemed to be in charge. I had no idea. All the meatheads looked the same to me."

"Where have you taken her to fight in the past?" Finn asked. "The places change, but maybe there's a pattern."

Dustin used his phone's mapping system to share pins from several of the fight locations with Finn.

His expression fell, apparently not seeing a pattern.

"When was the next time you were supposed to drive her?" Finn asked.

"Tomorrow night."

He pulled the notebook from his pocket and confirmed the time. "It's a match."

Hope rushed through Josi's body. Today would be the last day of this nightmare.

Chapter Twenty

Josi bumbled her way through the next workday, sliding back into her role as stable manager while Lincoln worked with the horses and other ranch hands. Community Days on the ranch were a big deal to the Beaumonts, and she needed to keep her head in the game. Finn and his team had a plan for tonight, and members of Marshal's Bluff PD were already searching the most rural areas for signs of Tara.

In a few hours, she would be safe. The fight club would be dismantled. The perpetrators, gunmen and abductors in jail.

Josi just had to keep smiling and answering equine-related questions a little longer.

The sun shone brightly outside her office window, almost warm enough to burn away the gloom and fear from her heart. Almost. Children's laughter danced in the wind. Happy voices chatted in the stables and on the ranch grounds. She normally loved these events, but congeniality and joy wouldn't come easily today. Not until she knew Tara was safe.

Lincoln's steady footfalls echoed on the stable floor, growing significantly louder as they got near.

She turned to watch the open doorway until he appeared.

A smile tugged his lips when their eyes met. "Hey."

"Hey."

He slid inside and looked her over.

Shafts of light through her slatted blinds illuminated his tanned skin in stripes, leaving a deep shadow over his face and hiding his moss-green eyes. His boots and jeans were muddy from hoisting kids onto horseback and leading them along the preset paths he'd designed for Community Days. His cologne mixed with fresh air and dried hay in ways that made her stomach tumble.

"How are you holding up?" he asked.

"I'm okay." She shrugged. "Trying to stay busy. Keep my mind off of things. You?"

He nodded then took a step in her direction, pausing to lean against her desk. "Finn called. His men are doing surveillance along the harbor now. Things are quiet, but if this is a fight night, it'll be the last."

Josi released a long shaky breath, willing his words to be true. Finn was good at his job. He was smart and lev-elheaded. Tara would be safe in his hands. Now, Josi just needed to convince herself to relax.

"Dad and the ranch hands are moving the horses into the big field for a little show. Food's being lined up on the tables for lunch. You should come out and get a bite," Lincoln said.

Josi shook her head. "I don't think I can face your family or a crowd. The Beaumonts will all see through me, right down to my shaking boots. The crowd will only make me nervous."

Lincoln opened his arms and tented his eyebrows in question.

She went to him in a heartbeat, falling easily into his embrace.

Strong arms circled her, gathering her close, and she in-haled the precious scents of her personal guardian, friend and love. "Wow, I needed this," she whispered, rising onto tiptoes and snuggling deeper into his protective hold.

"Do you also need food?" he asked. "I can smuggle a couple of plates in here and have a little lunch with you."

Josi groaned at the perfection of his offer. "Yes. Please." It was as if she'd been craving his nearness and hadn't really put a finger on the need until he'd said the words. "Are you sure you can get away for a lunch break?"

Lincoln pulled back and scoffed.

"Right." She smiled. "You do what you want."

"And so do you," he assured her. "Now, what can I get you from the tables?"

A familiar country song began outside, signaling a new event and meant to move visitors in the right direction.

Josi loosened her hold on Lincoln, feeling better, if a little guilty for tying up his time. Nowhere near guilty enough to turn him down. "I would love a burger and baked macaroni and cheese, if it's out there. I've got water in here." She pointed to the mini fridge in the corner. "Maybe something sweet too?"

His mouth ticked up in a mischievous half smile and he pressed a kiss to her lips. "Be right back."

A set of gunshots exploded in the distance, and Josi's heart seized.

Then the screaming began.

"Stay here," Lincoln said. "Call 911, then Finn."

The door slammed shut, taking her view of him with it. Josi's heart hammered.

She snapped into action, grabbing her phone with uncoordinated fingers and searching for Lincoln in the mess outside her window. She took in the chaos as she dialed.

Spooked horses rose onto hind legs. Young riders fell to the ground. People scrambled to save the fallen, or ran away to save themselves. An equine stampede ran through the panicked crowd. Food tables were overturned. Truck alarms went off.

"Come on," she whispered, willing the call to connect.

"Ah, ah, ah," a low voice chided.

Gooseflesh pebbled her skin, and she spun toward the sound. The barbs of a Taser shot into her chest, jolting her silent before a leather-gloved hand covered her mouth and dragged her away.

LINCOLN SPRINTED OUTSIDE, senses on high alert and instincts kicking him into gear. "Dad!" he called, catching sight of his father on the ground near a kneeling woman and small child.

"Settle the horses!" his dad returned. "Get folks out of the way."

Lincoln changed directions, scooping a toddler off the ground and passing her to a confused-looking teen. "Take her to the porch and keep her there," he barked. "Take as many others as you can. Go!"

The teen blinked, then jolted forward, taking the hand of another child as he began to dash toward the farmhouse.

In the distance, sirens rang out. He thanked his lucky stars for Josi's call to emergency services and for the help that was on the way. Horses were gentle giants until they were afraid. Then they were frantic babies. Too large for their own good, and too dangerous for anyone unprepared.

The ranch hands slowed a few of the younger animals, then swung themselves onto the saddles. Not an easy trick, but a skill Lincoln could appreciate. Especially when those same people used the mounted horses to catch and corral the others.

A desperate wail redirected his attention to a man on the ground. He was cradling a young woman's head on his lap. Her eyes were closed. Crimson stained her blond hair, the man's shirt and hands as he struggled to slow the blood flow. A matching stain on a nearby rock suggested she'd fallen, probably from a horse, and knocked herself unconscious. "Help!" the man called, eyes searching frantically. "We need a doctor!"

Lincoln skidded to a stop two feet away. "Ambulances are en route. What's your name?"

"Frank."

"Frank," Lincoln repeated. "Who's this?"

"My daughter. Emma." The man choked on her name. "We brought her out to see the ranch. She's struggling at home, but… We thought the ranch would be good for her. She didn't want to come." He squeezed his eyelids shut, and a tear appeared on his cheek.

In the distance, the ranch hands returned several horses to a gated pen. Ambulances trundled along the gravel driveway, avoiding frightened people and exiting vehicles.

Lincoln's chest tightened unexpectedly. Images of injured soldiers flashed in his memory. Fear and tension that should've been left on the other side of the world pressed into his mind, stealing his breath and stilling his limbs.

He pushed against the intrusive thoughts, bringing better, more recent memories to the forefront of his mind. Josi speaking softly, confidently. Her small hands on his cheeks or chest. Promising everything was okay.

"Everything is going to be okay, Frank," he said, voice unnaturally low. He waved a hand high overhead, catching a medic's eye. "Talk to Emma. Let her know you're here and not to be afraid. Then explain exactly what happened to the medic."

Frank nodded and began speaking to his unconscious daughter.

Lincoln clapped the EMT on the back as he arrived. "Head injury."

The medic dropped into a squat beside Frank.

Lincoln moved on to the next set of people curled on the grass. "Wait on the porch," he told a set of young boys positioned on their knees, heads down and hands folded over top.

"A shooter!" one boy cried. "There's a gun."

Lincoln scanned the scene. Dazed people wandered the grounds, calling out to friends and family.

"That's my mom!" a second boy exclaimed, jumping to his feet.

"Go," Lincoln ordered. "All of you. Up!"

The boys stood, then ran.

The shooter, however, was nowhere to be found.

And no one seemed to have been shot.

His gaze snapped to the stable, then to Josi's office window. She wasn't there. He'd been sure she would be watching, relaying the details to Finn or a dispatcher by phone. Maybe even looking for him.

He turned in a slow circle, hoping she hadn't wandered into the chaos, where she would be vulnerable to attack. Then, suddenly, he understood.

The gunfire wasn't intended to cause harm. Each shot had done exactly what it was meant to do. And Lincoln had reacted precisely as expected.

He'd left Josi alone.

He was in motion before the thought had finished forming. "Look out," he called, dodging guests as they crisscrossed the field. "Move!"

His chest ached with effort as he leaped over abandoned bags and toppled strollers on his way to the stable. He sucked in his first full breath of hope as a familiar figure came into view outside Josi's office.

"Mama!" He slowed upon approach. "You okay?"

She nodded, eyes wide and expression aghast. "I am. I saw you in the field, and I came to check on Josi."

"Same." He nodded, pressing a hand to the pinch in his side. "She's all right?" he asked, following his mama's gaze through the open door.

"I don't know," she said. "I haven't seen her."

Lincoln froze beside his mother, gaze fixed on the empty office before them.

Josi was gone.

Chapter Twenty-One

Josi woke to harsh light and a shooting pain through her forehead. She blinked to clear her vision, trying and failing to gain her bearings.

"Be still," a rough male voice commanded.

The jostling of a vehicle slowly registered, and she struggled again to focus her eyes. "Where are we?" she croaked.

"Shut up," the man snapped. "Keep your head down."

She let the words settle in her addled mind. Why was she so confused?

She'd been in her office, watching from the window as the Beaumonts and farm hands slowed the horses and tended to the frantic crowd. She'd seen Lincoln speaking with a man beside an injured young woman.

Then—

A low groan rolled through her as she opened her eyes once more. When had they closed? Her gaze slid from the bright southern sun to the unfamiliar dashboard and interior. Black on black. Scents of heady cologne and leather.

Her throat was dry as she swallowed, her head pounded as she attempted to turn or lift it away from the window at her side.

Something hard pressed against her hip.

"I said do not move." The man ground out each word.

And Josi's heart began to race, adrenaline slowly burning away the haze of whatever had happened to her.

She tried again to remember the moments at her office window and failed.

Sirens wailed as she rocked in the unfamiliar vehicle. *Emergency vehicles*, she realized. Help was headed to the farm. A measure of relief swept through her along with choppy memories of injured guests. And a gunman.

Breath caught in her throat as the recollection of unexpected gunshots sloshed in her soggy mind. Suddenly, the hard press against her thigh took new shape, registering as the barrel of a gun.

The vehicle picked up speed as it passed the parade of ambulances and police cruisers, their sirens growing faint. Her driver released a long, laborious sigh. "I thought we'd never get away from that damn ranch."

Josi leaned herself upright, forcing her muscles to cooperate as she sat tall. The Beaumont Ranch shrank quickly in the mirror outside her window.

She rode on the front passenger seat of a black SUV, piloted by Dennis Cane, the Barbell Club manager.

His angry brown eyes slid her way briefly before returning to the road. "You just can't take a hint. Won't follow instructions. Make everything unnecessarily difficult." He jammed the gun painfully against her hip, causing her to wince.

Her body was heavy, as if underwater. "Where are we going?" she asked, voice thick and sounding foreign to her own ears.

"Somewhere you can't cause any more trouble," he said. "I've got a business to run and people counting on these fights. Your sweet little-girl-next-door look will bring a pretty penny. I can think of more than a few men who'd pay to see you taken down. A handful who'd like to do the job themselves."

"Why?" she croaked, unable to clear the gravel from her voice.

"Because you look like everything they hate in a woman." He chuckled. "And I can't say I disagree. We had to put the show on pause the last time things went sideways. I'm not ready to do that again. Taking you out of the equation should fix things up nicely."

"Again?" she asked, her mind working more quickly than her lips. Hadn't the fight club been dismantled fully after Marcus's death?

"Yeah. A lot of good men went to prison the last time. Too many. You can't even imagine the amount of money I lost while things were on hold. I won't let that happen again. They're lucky to have me at the helm."

A lot of good men went to prison the last time. But not Dennis Cane, and he had been in charge.

He pulled the gun away and rested it on his thigh.

"Do you have Tara?" she asked, a boulder of fear in her throat. "Can I see her?"

"Absolutely. You can braid one another's hair and have a little reunion before showtime. After that, you're mine."

A violent shiver rocked down her spine. Josi didn't want to know what he'd meant by that. Every possibility made her equally sick. She had to concentrate and regain her strength if she wanted to escape with Tara. Until then, she could only hope Finn and his men knew where tonight's fight would occur.

The vehicle hit a pothole, and her gaze bounced around the interior once more. A rag on the floor at her feet set off a series of rapid-fire memories.

She'd been at the window when Dennis entered her office—

he'd shot her with a Taser then dragged her away. When he'd covered her mouth with a rag, the scent had been sickly sweet, then the world had gone dark. "You drugged me," she whispered. It would explain her memory loss, heavy limbs and searing headache. "You're the one who caused a panic at the ranch. You shot at Tara outside the motel." All of the week's most horrible events returned in a rush. "You sent those cars to chase us. Sent the men to interrogate Bella and try to take me."

"You know what they say," he said. "If you want something done right...do it yourself."

She rolled her eyes, and pain shot through her skull. Uncoordinated hands fumbled to pat her pockets.

"I took your phone," he said. "If that's what you're looking for, I tossed it out before we got into the truck. No one's saving you from the tower, princess. Or in your case, the dungeon."

Josi sank back against the seat, head lolling and gaze moving through the glass at her side. Familiar scenery blurred past. Shops and trees. Traffic and pedestrians. People going cheerfully about their days while she sat quietly hostage. Even if she could find the strength to scream, she was certain her body hadn't recovered enough to get away. And if she somehow managed the impossible, what would happen to Tara?

The world blinked in and out until the vehicle finally stopped, and Josi's eyes opened once more.

Dennis closed the driver's-side door with a jarring thud. Moments later, a wave of salty air crashed over her.

Something soft covered her face and she gasped.

The world went dark once more.

"Josi." Someone nearby spoke her name. "Wake up." Her cheek stung, and her eyelids fluttered open.

Her stomach twisted and coiled. Metallic scents churned in the dry, earthy air.

"Hey…" The voice came again, familiar this time, though brittle and thin. "You have to move," the woman said. "They'll be back soon."

Fresh panic and fear scratched at Josi's mind.

"Lincoln," she whispered, the name rolling off her tongue. Was he okay? Where was he now?

An arm locked with hers and pulled her upright, turning Josi until her head and back rested against a rough stone wall. Her bottom pressed against a cool, hard floor. Before her, a blurry figure came into focus.

Tears spilled over the younger woman's swollen cheeks and cracked lips. Her beautiful blue eyes were red with busted blood vessels. Her body was battered and bruised.

"Tara." Josi opened her arms and pulled her friend into a hug. A hot rush of tears made her vision temporarily worse.

Tara held her tight, body shaking with silent sobs.

"Are you okay?" Josi asked, hoping Tara felt better than she looked. "What happened to you?"

"Dennis," Tara said, rocking back on her haunches before falling onto the floor with a sharp cry.

"I've been looking for you since that night at the hotel. The police are too. What's going on?"

Tara glanced over her shoulder, then back to Josi, swallowing hard before speaking once more. "I overheard a few guys talking about gambling at a party. It sounded as if they were betting on fights, and I thought of Marcus. I tried to get information, but they shut me out. I worried about the possibility of another fight club, so I asked more questions. At first, I couldn't find anyone willing to talk. Then I saw a woman leaving the Barbell Club, while I was waiting for the guys to come out. I'd planned to follow them when they left, but I followed her instead. She had two black eyes and peeled away from the lot like the place was on fire. When she stopped for gas, I approached. She was discreet, but everything she said seemed to confirm my fear."

"The fight club is running again," Josi said, pulling her jumbled thoughts into line.

Tara nodded. "The woman was a single mom who'd started fighting for extra money, and it gave me an idea." Tears rolled over her cheeks as she spoke, and she hissed with pain when she brushed them away. Her hand was gnarled and wrapped with tape, and was probably broken. "I thought I could get inside and bring down the ring for good. I wanted to get names and evidence I could turn over to the police department. Especially the person in charge. If I don't stop him, the club will keep making a comeback."

"That's when you started training at Bella's," Josi said, the missing pieces coming together.

Surprise crossed Tara's face at the mention of the gym owner. "How did you—"

"We met her. She's been helping us." Josi motioned for Tara to sit at her side, and the younger woman obeyed. Josi leaned against her shoulder, willing her thoughts to clear and her limbs to regain strength and coordination.

"We?" Tara asked, tipping her head against Josi. "Not Dennis."

"No, the Beaumonts. Lincoln and Finn, mostly. Finn's a detective. The whole family has been doing what they can to help find you. And they're going to make sure this fight club comes down for the last time. We just have to help them find us when they get here." Josi looked more carefully at the dim space around them, listened to the sounds of rain against a metal roof. "Where are we?" And when had it started to rain? How long had she been unconscious?

"The old grain mill near the harbor," Tara said. "All the money goes through here, and it's where they keep the fighters too injured to get home on their own."

Josi grimaced. "Like you."

"I don't get to go home, because they know what I was up to. I won't leave here alive."

"Don't talk like that." Anger mixed with adrenaline in Josi's heart and mind. "You will survive this. We're both leaving this place tonight. The minute I can stand on my own."

"I can't," Tara said, voice cracking again. "They make me fight every night until I'm out cold and don't get back up. Just like Marcus. My head never has time to heal. My body's broken." She pressed curled hands against her face to quiet her sobs.

Josi's arm went around her friend and pulled her gently closer. "I need you to fight one more time. Okay? Fight with me to get out of here."

LINCOLN SAT AT the kitchen table with his family, reviewing multiple security feeds from around the Beaumont property. The ranch often housed troubled teens, and that required knowing everything that went on, as well as having the ability to find kids who occasionally tried to sneak away. They'd rarely needed to review more than one feed at a time, but the system had the capability, and they'd put it to use.

Dean and Austin had shown up to help in any way they could. And like the rest of the family, they were exceptional at their jobs. Their assistance was priceless.

Now, everyone had a laptop and a security feed to analyze in the hopes of spotting Josi and the direction she'd been taken.

Lincoln's mama refilled everyone's mugs with coffee before she took a seat beside their father and linked her arm with his. He kissed her head without looking away from the feed. The simple gestures of love and support hit Lincoln in the chest like an anvil.

He hadn't dared to want what his parents had in a long time, but getting closer to Josi had brought those old dreams back to the forefront. He knew now, without any doubt, the only future he wanted had her in it.

"We'll find her," his mother whispered, reaching one hand across the table to pat his wrist.

Something hot and wet slid along his face, and he rubbed it hastily away. It took a long moment for him to realize he was crying.

All eyes locked on him as he inhaled, then released a shaky breath. "I love her," he admitted. Hating that the one woman he wanted was the only one his parents wouldn't want for him. A woman they already saw as a member of the family, and one they probably thought was way too young.

Their collective expressions turned pitying instead of the shock or horror he'd expected. His brothers shook their heads and frowned.

"About time you figured that out," Austin said flatly, returning his attention to the screen before him. "Y'all have been driving us up the wall with the goo-goo eyes and the pining for a year."

"At least that long." Dean snorted a laugh, already back to reviewing the security feed.

Lincoln blinked, too stunned to speak as he searched Finn's and his parents' faces. "What?"

"We know," Finn said, waving a hand around, indicating the whole team. "We talk about it all the time."

Lincoln pressed back in his seat. "How do you know?"

His mother made a low humming noise that sounded like a wordless "bless your heart." "Sweetie. We have eyes."

Lincoln frowned. "You're not mad."

"Why on earth would we be mad?" his father asked.

"We're delighted," his mama said. "She's strong and smart. And she seems to love you too."

"You don't see her as a part of the family? A daughter?" he asked his folks. "Or a sister?" He turned to his brothers.

Dean wrinkled his nose. "Alison, Hayley and Scarlet are part of the family now," Dean said. "That's the point, isn't it?"

Austin smirked. "What's important is that you don't see her as a sister."

Lincoln rubbed heavy palms against his face, joy mixing with heartbreak in his soul. "I can't believe I left her alone. Now, she's gone, and we don't have the first clue where to find her."

"Well," his dad said, attention fixed to the screen. "I might."

Chairs scraped over wooden floorboards as Lincoln and his brothers rose in quick unison. They moved to stand behind their parents and examine his father's security feed. Dennis Cane from the Barbell Club came into view, moving from the stable to a waiting SUV, a slumping woman at his side. He tucked her into the passenger's side and drove away, passing incoming emergency responders.

Chapter Twenty-Two

Shafts of waning daylight poured through cracks in ancient walls, slowly changing from the warm gold of an autumn day to the cool periwinkle of twilight. Wind whistled between the bricks, stirring up dirt on the cracked concrete floor. In the distance, thunder rolled.

Josi made her way around the room's perimeter, leaning against the wall for support as needed. She grew stronger and steadier by the minute, which was good, because according to Tara, they didn't have much time. She pressed her toe and shoulder to brick and wallboard, then raised a cast-off piece of metal to test the air ducts and ceiling beams.

"Once it gets dark, they'll announce the fight schedule and start taking bets. Then they'll come for us," Tara said.

Josi stilled. "What do you mean?" She vaguely remembered Dennis saying he wanted her in the ring, but Tara could barely walk. "They can't expect you to fight again tonight," she said.

Tara offered a sad smile. "They do. And I will. At least until I'm knocked out again. I just hope they don't pit us against one another."

"Never," Josi said, impossibly more horrified. She wouldn't hit anyone, especially not someone as injured as Tara. And never Tara.

"You'd be surprised what they can make us do." Tara cast her gaze to the floor, face paling with unspoken thoughts.

Josi doubled down on the task at hand. She slid the tip of the metal between slats in a vent just out of reach, then angled it like a pry bar.

The frantic shrieking of mice echoed overhead.

"They're in the vents," Tara said. "They fall out at night."

Josi moved close to the wall, peering in the direction of the now distant sounds. "How do they get in there?"

"I have no idea." Tara sagged to the floor. "I guess the vents lead somewhere outside, or at least into another part of the mill."

"Get up," Josi said, a new idea forming. Neither of them were in any condition to fight tonight, but maybe they were strong enough to follow the mice.

"What are you doing?" Tara asked, stumbling to Josi's side. Her noticeable limp and occasionally slurred speech seemed to be getting worse.

"Give me a boost." Josi moved under the vent and out-stretched her arms. "I only need a few inches."

Tara lowered to her hands and knees. "I can't balance well enough to squat, but you can stand on my back."

"Perfect." Josi stepped gingerly onto her friend, cringing at Tara's resulting whimper. She slid her fingers through the slats in the grate and tugged. Two of the corner screws fell out, landing on the ground beneath her. She worked the final two with her thumb and forefinger until they were removed as well. "Okay." Josi climbed down and set the grate on the ground. Then she offered Tara her hand. "Put me on your shoulders. I'll climb into the vent and pull you up after me."

An eternity later, when both women were past exhaustion, and night had fully fallen, Josi finally dragged Tara into the vent.

They let the mice lead the way.

Moving along on their stomachs, Josi and Tara wiggled like snakes in the cramped space, too short to rise onto hands and knees. The air was dank and uncomfortable, and the mice were only inches from Josi's face.

"I can't see," Tara said, slapping her hand against Josi's foot for the dozenth time. "Sorry."

"Me either, but we're making progress. Whatever you do, don't stop moving, and we'll be there soon," she encouraged.

"Where?"

"I don't know," she admitted. But anywhere was better than where they were and where they'd been.

Spiderwebs crisscrossed the vents, catching across Josi's face and making her want to scream. But drawing unwanted attention was something she couldn't afford. When she placed a hand in something warm and wet, she told herself not to think about what it might have been. The only thing that mattered was getting Tara to safety.

"I see light," Josi whispered, moving as quickly as possible through the metal shaft. The vent took a sharp left, but straight ahead was a way out. She reached the grate over a small office and peered inside. The room was empty, but a desk lamp illuminated the space. She slid her fingers through the metal slats, gripped the bars and pushed, but the grate didn't move. She tried again, using the full force of her arms, until the bottom corner gave way. One metal screw hit the floor with a clink, then began to roll.

In the distance, male voices registered and grew loud.

Tara tugged Josi's ankles. Her curled fingers scratched at Josi's leg. "That's them," she whispered, the words hushed but frantic. "Stop."

Josi inched backward, and Tara made room. Seconds

later, a trio of large shadows entered the little office, climbing the walls like monsters.

Dennis took a seat in the creaky office chair. "Get the girls," he said casually. "Take them both to the ring. We'll let the new one watch the other one get her teeth kicked in. I want them to regret testing me. When we toss the blonde in the ring after that, she'll be too scared to move. If she cries and begs to get out, all the better."

"Fresh meat," someone said on a chuckle. "Folks will throw money at that."

"Sure," a third man said, mild concern in his tone. "Until they're dead. Then we've got bodies to bury."

"Harbor is right there," Dennis said. "And this town needs a warning. There'll be more deaths to follow if everyone doesn't stay out of my business."

Josi pressed her lips tight against the urge to be sick.

"Let's go," he said. "I'm eager to get started."

The office emptied. It would only be a matter of minutes before the men looking for Josi and Tara realized they were gone. Additional seconds before they saw the vent's grate on the ground and knew exactly how to find them.

Josi angled around the corner, moving into the adjoining vent on her left. Tara followed. Their quiet shimmies seemed to make gonging sounds against the metal.

She paused at the next light source and reached quickly for the grate. When the cover didn't move, she backed up and carried on, eager to find a fast escape.

Inaudible voices and booming footfalls echoed in the distance beneath them, reaching up from the old grain mill to Josi's ears.

"I think they realized we're gone," Tara said, voice dazed and dreamy in a way that raised Josi's already frantic heart rate.

"We have to keep moving," she whispered. The men would be in the vents soon, assuming they could fit, or maybe they'd spread out, one in every room, waiting for her and Tara to reappear. Either way wouldn't end well. "You doing okay back there?"

Tara grunted softly, her curled hands bumping against Josi's feet as they moved.

"Another room." Josi hurried forward, pushing against the next grate. It moved immediately. A second hard shove set it free. Josi launched forward, chasing after the heavy cover, catching it by a single crooked finger before it crashed onto the concrete floor.

Tara caught Josi around her legs, torso pressed against the backs of her thighs, holding her in place as she hung, head first, over an empty room.

Tears fell from Josi's eyes, running down her forehead and into her hair as she struggled to catch a full breath. "Thank you."

Before she was ready, she reached downward, stretching toward the floor. Tara kept her from a free fall—she was trembling, but holding tight to her legs. Josi released the grate gently, careful not to make a sound, then planted her palms against the floor. A moment later, she collapsed onto the ground in a messy heap.

Tara's head and shoulders appeared above her, extended from the vent.

Josi rose to help her down.

Angry male voices filled the building, shouting threats and laments. The sounds echoed from every corner. Their footfalls pounded, sneakers squeaking against the uncarpeted floors.

"Hurry," Josi ordered, wrapping her arms around Tara as she pulled the remainder of her body free.

They stumbled and fell back with a soft thud and muted groans.

"You okay?" Josi asked, moving onto her hands and knees, then pushing upright to stand.

Tara's face was red and contorted in pain. "My hands are broken. My fingers and wrists. Ribs too, I think? Or bruised."

Josi bent to help her upright, hating that she hadn't asked about the extent of her friend's injuries sooner. It was easy to see she wasn't well, but she hadn't asked any questions. The words *I'm sorry* sat on her tongue, but there wasn't any time for that now. They needed to get out of the building. They needed to get Tara somewhere safe.

Before they reached the door, gunshots rang out. A distinct tearing of metal told the rest of the story.

The men were shooting into the vents.

LINCOLN LEAPED FROM the passenger side of Finn's truck before it'd stopped moving. He reached the Barbell Club's door as Dean pulled in behind them, Austin at his side. The lot was empty, save a single white hatchback and black truck that looked as if it hadn't moved in decades.

"Lincoln," Finn called, his truck door slamming shut, as if to underscore his authority. "Wait for me."

The lights were off inside the building. A list of hours posted on the glass indicated the business was closed.

Lincoln tried the door anyway. "Locked." He raised a fist and pounded hard, then cupped both hands around his eyes to peer inside. "This gym is open late six days a week. Today it closed early. Three guesses as to why."

Dean and Austin moved into line beside Finn, all facing Lincoln.

Dean was next to speak. "We know the SUV caught

leaving the ranch on the security feed is registered to a company who also owns this gym," Dean said.

Finn had run the plate immediately.

"Is there somewhere else we can look for Dennis Cane?" Dean asked. "Maybe someone else who works here and might have answers? Some other way to cover our bases?"

Finn dragged his attention from the phone in his hand to Dean. "I don't know. I sent a cruiser to his home on our way here. The officer says no one was there. No signs of the truck in the neighborhood." He tucked the phone into his pocket, jaw locked in frustration.

Lincoln bit the insides of his cheeks to keep from screaming. He assured himself that breaking every window of the gym behind him, operated by a woman-abducting, illegal-fight-club-running criminal, wouldn't help either. Though it would be incredibly satisfying. "What now?" he asked.

The fact that Josi had been taken so brazenly from his family ranch didn't bode well for her safety. Dennis Cane had taken a major risk. He wanted her silenced.

And time was ticking.

Finn retrieved his phone, expression expectant as he looked at the device, then pressed it to his ear. "Detective Beaumont." His gaze slid to Lincoln. "That's all we need. Get the warrant." He disconnected with a smirk. "Ballistics matched casings found at the ranch to those pulled from a tree used for target practice on Cane's property. Combine that with Josi's abduction and the vehicle leaving the scene of the crime, we won't have any problem getting a warrant to search the gym and his home. Wherever he's holding Tara and Josi, we'll find them."

Lincoln stepped away, needing space to think. "What about the men you're tailing?" Lincoln asked. "Any word on them?"

Finn tapped his phone screen and initiated the speaker function. "Let's check in."

"Ramos," a deep male voice answered.

"Hey," Finn said. "Where's your guy?"

"Heading along the scenic byway. I'm a few cars back, but he's not even looking. He's been running some kind of errands all day. On the move since lunch. I'm starving."

Austin chuckled.

Finn sighed. "Have you talked to the others?"

"Yeah," Ramos said, a little more brightly. "They're moving this way. Their guys are on the byway too."

Lincoln straightened, watching as his brothers figured out what he had. "It's fight night." Everyone involved was likely heading to the location Lincoln and Finn had been searching for.

"Where are you now, precisely?" Finn asked.

"Passing mile marker eleven, out near the old grain mill."

"That's only a mile or so from where that woman found Tara walking," Lincoln said.

Finn circled a hand in the air as he turned for his truck.

The brothers raced to their rides. Within seconds, they were back in play, and Lincoln's gut said this was it. The area near the old grain mill would make the perfect location for a group to gather outside, and the mill itself would be a good place to hide a pair of hostages. No amount of screaming would be heard so far from everything and everyone else.

Minutes later, Finn slowed as he turned onto a narrow path through the field toward the old mill. The road had grown over with weeds and grass. In the distance, vehicles had begun to gather. He tapped the screen of his truck and relayed what he saw to Dispatch, who assured him that backup was on the way. Ramos and the others who'd been tailing Dennis Cane's men took strategic positions and awaited Finn's word.

Lincoln gripped the handle on his door, ready to jump out again.

Finn raised one palm in warning and frowned to underscore the silent order. *Be still and stay put.*

Behind them, Dean's truck crawled to a stop as well.

Finn disconnected with Dispatch and dialed Ramos. "What can you see from your vantage?"

"We're in the field. Just paid to park, but the money man was tight-lipped about what I was parking to see."

"Hold your position," Finn said. "Keep me posted. Backup is a few minutes out. We're going to take a closer look at the mill on foot."

Lincoln opened his door and met his brothers outside. Finn looked each of them in the eye for a long beat before turning toward the mill. They'd all seen that look before. Their little brother was in cop mode, and it was best to fall in line.

Together, they flanked their leader and marched steadily toward their target.

A sudden burst of gunfire sent them into a collective crouch, trading looks before realizing the shots hadn't been fired at their approach. The sounds had come from inside the mill.

And just like that, they launched into a sprint with Lincoln leading the charge.

Chapter Twenty-Three

Josi grabbed Tara by the hand and pulled, snapping her into motion. They needed to get away from the building before the shooter realized they weren't in the vents anymore.

Tara stumbled forward on unsteady legs, knocking into a small metal trash can and toppling it onto the floor. She froze, free hand extended as if to right the bin.

"Leave it," Josi hissed. "We have to go."

They slipped through the office door and into a hallway, their shoes padding softly against the ground. Every sound was magnified in the massive, abandoned building, carrying down corridors and through the sprawling space. Thankfully, the shooting had stopped.

Josi towed Tara along, checking regularly over her shoulder.

Tara's pace slowed by a fraction with every step. Her gait grew awkward and inconsistent. She cradled one arm across her chest, wincing repeatedly, expression contorted. She was filthy and bruised from head to toe, her clothes smeared with blood.

Her normally soft hair was slick from days without a wash. And a cut on her mouth had opened and begun to bleed. How many times had Tara been carried away from the ring this week, then tossed into the cellar until the next fight? Not that she could possibly fight in her condition. She doubted Tara could even stand for long on her own. Yet the men were coming to get her.

The vents above them groaned, and Josi refocused on the escape. Tara likely wouldn't survive another fight, and neither she nor Josi would survive long if they got in front of a bullet.

"I see blood!" a male voice boomed. The sound seemed to come from the ceiling.

Had the cut on Tara's mouth opened while they were in the vents? Were they leaving a trail?

A moment later, the sound of an opening door sent them into a jog.

Tara whimpered and switched to a hop, no longer able to keep up on her more injured leg.

Panic welled in Josi as she searched for a place to hide. She pulled Tara through the next open doorway, praying for boxes or furniture to duck behind. Instead, they found themselves on a metal landing overlooking a two-story section of the mill—they were fully exposed. A dozen metal steps stood between them and the old machinery, their only chance to hide.

Beside her, Tara's hand went limp, and her body slowly slumped to the floor.

LINCOLN MOVED CAREFULLY into the old grain mill, measuring his steps while Finn took the lead with his badge and gun. Lincoln would've preferred ripping the door off its ancient hinges instead of creeping, but he knew the drill. This was a reconnaissance mission first. Tearing the place down, metaphorically, came second.

The interior was large and dank. Scents of oil and earth hung in the air. Large, motionless machinery stood before them on a cement floor. Two stories of small black-painted windows rose to the metal rafters. An office with a large viewing space faced the floor across from a set of steps that overlooked it all.

Dennis Cane stood inside the office, attention fixed on a metal landing atop the stairs. Two familiar figures sat motionless in his sights. Dennis raised one extended arm, a gun in hand. The barrel was pointed at Josi and Tara.

"No!" The word ripped from Lincoln's chest.

Dennis swung around with a start and pulled the trigger. Bang!

The Beaumonts ducked, and Dennis fled.

"Marshal's Bluff PD!" Finn called, tearing off in the gunman's direction.

"Josi's on the steps," Lincoln told Dean and Austin. "I think Tara's with her."

"Go," Austin said, nudging Dean in Finn's direction. "Cover Finn. We'll retrieve the hostages."

Lincoln broke into a jog. Numerous machines and conveyors filled the space and complicated his path. A second gunshot dropped him into a crouch.

The bullet dinged loudly off metal, indicating it had hit something close by.

Austin jumped behind a nearby machine. "I'll cover you."

Lincoln scanned the area for signs of the shooter, then continued toward the stairs. A fresh round of shots redirected him once more.

"Go!" Austin called, slipping back into view, sidearm in hand.

Sometimes belonging to a family of armed lawmen and private eyes had real perks.

A trickle of blood on the floor caught Lincoln's attention. He tracked the pattern of small sporadic dots to a wall of decrepit boxes stacked six feet high. He rushed forward, head down and body low as bullets zinged and crashed around him.

The nearby click of a cocking gun froze him in his spot. A man he recognized from the Barbell Club stepped into full view, a sneer on his face and a revolver in his hand.

The last time Lincoln had seen the man, he'd been in a boxing ring with someone half a foot taller, pretending to have no idea Dennis Cane was a killer.

"Must be my lucky day," the guy said. "You're just what we need to fish these women out from hiding. After that, maybe we'll finally see if you can box."

Lincoln appraised the man's distance and grip on the weapon. He could disarm him with a little distraction. "You lost your hostages?" Lincoln's heart soared with pride. Josi must've been terrified, but she was never a victim. He laughed, and the man scowled. "They outsmarted you, right? I mean, it probably didn't take much."

The man's expression morphed from confusion to offense, but before he could raise his gun, the wall of boxes beside them came crashing down.

A cloud of dust and grain rose into the air, and Lincoln lurched forward, knocking the weapon from the other man's hand. He shoved him back several paces, but the man bent forward, ran for Lincoln's middle and threw him to the hard ground with a bone-rattling thud.

Gunshots continued in the mill as Austin kept another shooter at bay.

It was on Lincoln to knock this one out and find Josi.

A blond blur rushed around him as he struck his opponent in the jaw and received a jab to his already sore ribs. They rolled and tussled, trading blows and each of them working to gain the upper hand.

An earsplitting gunshot froze them in place, too close to ignore.

Josi widened her stance, pistol raised overhead. "Stop!"

The man lifted his palms. Blood streamed from his nose, and one eye had begun to swell. Lincoln would've preferred that number to be two.

He winked at Josi. "Attagirl."

Silence suddenly reigned in the cavernous building, disrupted only by the growing wails of sirens outside.

"Help me get her out of here," Josi said, motioning to the pile of fallen boxes.

Tara Stone appeared on unsteady legs, hobbling and bleeding from her lips and hands. She barely resembled the photos in her home. Both wrists had been taped for fighting. Her fingers had curled into broken claws. She favored one leg and pressed an arm to her middle.

Anger over what she'd been put through boiled inside him. "Hi, Tara," he said softly. "I'm Lincoln, and this is over."

At the top of the stairs, Finn walked Dennis Cane onto the landing in handcuffs.

Across the huge room, Austin lifted his hands in victory. "Thug down."

Josi began to cry as she moved toward her friend. "Ambulances are coming. Let's get you out of here." She passed the gun to Lincoln, and reached for Tara.

The sound of another gunshot exploded and pain cut though his side. He turned his eyes to the crimson stain blooming on his shirt, then to the man seated a few feet away.

Josi had taken his pistol, but he'd clearly had another.

"Marshal's Bluff PD," Finn called, flying down the steps, gun raised. "Stop! You're under arrest."

The shooter smirked at Lincoln, but set his weapon on the ground.

Lincoln strode toward the shooter, and knocked him out.

"All right," Finn said, shoving Lincoln back. He kicked the criminal's gun away and cuffed him. "You know you've been shot, right?"

"It's a flesh wound," he grumbled, pressing a hand to his side. "I've had worse."

"I'm sure you have," Finn said, glancing back at him. "I'm worried about me. You were shot on my watch. Now, who's going to save me from Mama?"

Lincoln snorted a laugh, then swore through the pain.

The large metal door across the room opened, and men and women in uniforms filtered inside. Hurried footfalls and shouting voices raised his heart rate. A look at the wound beneath his shirt suddenly made him light-headed.

"Lincoln," Josi said, voice distant but heavy with concern.

He couldn't answer. His tongue was thick and his mouth dry, as the grain mill faded around him, replaced by ghosts from his past. Blood and chaos. Injured soldiers. Danger. Pain.

"Hey." Josi's face blurred into view. She pressed small, cool palms to his hot, stubbled cheeks. "I'm right here," she said. "We're together, and we're both okay." Tears spilled from her eyes, her voice cracking on every word. "The medics are coming. You're going to be just fine, but I need you to breathe."

He nodded woodenly, fighting to stay with her. "I'm so sorry," he croaked. "I let him get to you."

"No." She shook her head and pressed her lips to his when his body began to tremble. "Everything worked out," she promised. "Everyone is safe." She moved her hands away from his cheeks and pressed them to his side.

A roar of pain burst from his lips.

"Over here!" she called. "Help!"

Finn recited Miranda rights as medics arrived, medical bags in hand.

Dean and Austin bookended Josi, as paramedics loaded Lincoln onto a backboard beside Tara.

His teeth began to chatter with an overload of adrenaline searching for escape. "Josi."

"I'm here." She followed as they raised him onto a gurney, and she held his hand as they rushed him toward the mill's open door.

Moonlight illuminated the field full of emergency vehicles and officials.

A few yards away, Tara's eyes had gone shut.

Finn stuffed Dennis Cane into the back of a cruiser. "I'll meet y'all at the hospital," he called. "Let Josi ride with Lincoln. She's family."

The EMT nodded. He motioned to the set of open bay doors.

Lincoln's pounding heart wished more than anything that Finn's words were true. He wanted her to be a Beaumont. He wanted her as his wife.

The medic set an IV in Lincoln's arm and fixed an oxygen mask on his face once they were inside. "A little something for pain. Just breathe," he instructed.

Josi took a seat on his opposite side. "Ready," she said. "How're you doing?"

Lincoln pulled the mask away from his face. "I love you," he whispered, eyelids already pulling closed.

"I love you too," she promised. "Now put your mask on."

Epilogue

Six months later

Spring on the ranch was Lincoln's favorite time of year. There was something about the arrival of calves and foals, ducklings and every other kind of baby livestock that he absolutely loved. Not that he'd tell anyone other than Josi. It was true about friendly people getting extra attention, and the only person's attention he wanted in excess was Josi's.

He breathed in the warm evening air, admiring the remnants of a fading sunset and suppressing the mass of hope and excitement rising in his heart.

"What are you standing out here by yourself thinking about?" Josi asked. Her voice carried across the field as she made a path to his side.

They'd healed completely since their troubles in the fall, leaning on one another throughout the process. And they'd each found a professional counselor to talk to about unresolved issues in their pasts that might've otherwise stolen their joy in the future.

Even Tara was back on her feet. The doctors called her recovery miraculous, but from what Lincoln had seen and come to know about her, Tara was a fighter. He imagined there was little that could keep her down. She'd left her position at the pawnshop in favor of teaching classes at Body by Bella and seemed to be on an emotional healing journey of her own.

Best of all, her testimony had put Dennis Cane in jail for a very long time. A jury had found him guilty of a number of crimes, including kidnapping and attempted murder. They'd also found him complicit in the death of Marcus Stone. Several of Dennis's goons would remain behind bars nearly as long for similar reasons. And the illegal Marshal's Bluff fight club had finally, officially, been dismantled for good.

Josi stopped before him, smiling like she'd just been handed a prize. Blond hair hung over her shoulders in waves. The adorable sundress she'd chosen should've been illegal. Waning light backlit her sexy figure, and he imagined throwing her over his shoulder and taking her home. "Penny for your thoughts?"

Lincoln took her hand and pressed a kiss to her forehead, inhaling her sweet coconut scent. "You look beautiful."

Her mischievous blue eyes twinkled, and like every time they were this close, it felt like coming home.

His hands found the curves of her hips and pulled her closer, holding her body against his. He pressed his lips to her cheek and chin, then to the tip of her nose. When that wasn't enough, he went in for a proper kiss and took his time enjoying the stolen moment.

"Always dodging my questions," she said, a teasing smile on her lips. "But I will never complain about the way you distract me."

His lips quirked, but he fought back the smile. Josi made him happier than he'd ever dreamed of being, and each day with her had only gotten better. He was sure a lifetime with her would never be enough.

"What do you think of the dress?" she asked, stepping

back to spin in a small circle. The material floated around her thighs. She'd topped the simple sundress with a denim jacket and paired that with her pink-and-tan Western-style boots.

"Stunning," he assured her. "Like the smartest, toughest, kindest, prettiest cowgirl I've ever known."

Josi laughed softly. "I think I'll wear this more often."

The sound of tires on gravel turned her eyes in search of the arriving guest.

"Finn," she said. "We should say hi before we head out."

"Sounds good." He bit back a grin. "I need to stop at the stable first. We can catch Finn and my folks in a minute."

Josi turned happily on her heels and headed toward the large stable doors. She stopped to stare at the thin stream of light spilling along the ground outside. "Did someone leave the lights on?"

"Yep," Lincoln said, reaching for the metal handle and pulling it wide. "That was me."

JOSI SHOOK HER head as Lincoln pulled the doors open without unlocking them. He rarely forgot anything. To leave the lights on and the place unlocked was completely out of character. She'd definitely tease him about that later.

Her thoughts fizzled and her mind blanked as the stable's interior came into view. Strings of bistro lights hung in swoops from every rafter, and rose petals covered the floor. Lancelot snuffled and grunted in his stall, locking eyes with her as she entered.

"What is all this?" she asked, eyes and smile wide. It wasn't her birthday, or the anniversary of anything specific that she could recall.

She and Lincoln had been together almost six months, but they'd already made plans to celebrate that in a couple of weeks.

He tapped his phone screen and music played softly through a wireless speaker nearby. "Lincoln. This is gorgeous. I love it! And this my favorite song."

"You approve?" He pulled her close, his earthy cologne mixing with the familiar fragrances of wood and hay.

Lincoln raised their joined hands to his chest and draped her opposite arm over his shoulder. Then they began to sway.

"I've always wanted to slow-dance in the barn," she whispered, overwhelmed with immeasurable peace and joy. "I love that you remember the things I say, and that you pay attention to the things that are important to me," she said. "I hope I can make you half as happy someday."

A gentle rapping at the door caused her to turn and see Mr. and Mrs. Beaumont approach.

"Are we too late?" Mrs. Beaumont asked.

Lincoln shook his head, never missing a step in their dance. "Join us."

His mom covered her mouth briefly, eyes glistening with emotion as his father led her over the rose petals to a little space on the floor just for them. A few moments later, his brothers filed in, their wives and fiancées on their arms. Finn and Hayley, Dean and Nicole, Austin and Scarlet.

Josi batted away tears as her heart soared. The perfection of the moment was nearly more than she could bear. How had she come to be part of this big, goofy, loyal, loving family? And how had she been so lucky as to have them love her too?

The song ended, and the couples split, stepping apart to greet one another and admire the amazing, romantic decor.

"Tara's coming soon," Finn said. "She got off work a little late, but she's on her way."

Josi frowned. "Tonight?" Weren't she and Lincoln going out to dinner?

A hush rolled over the couples, and the women began to smile.

Josi followed their collective gaze to the space directly behind her, where Lincoln rested on one knee, a black velvet box in hand.

"Josi," he said, voice steady and strong. "I love you. I want to live a life at your side. Caring for animals, people and each other. I was wondering if you might want that too."

Tears clouded her eyes as she let his words pour over her. She hadn't thought it was possible for Lincoln to feel the same way she did, because she'd never felt like this before. "I do."

He opened the box and removed a diamond ring. Then he took her hand in his. "In that case, I hope you will consider doing me the incredible honor of being my wife."

"Yes," she rasped, heart soaring and tears falling.

He stood with a broad smile and spun her off her feet.

All around them, his family hooted and hollered.

Then someone pumped up the music.

The perfect beginning to a long, beautiful life together.

* * * * *

Be sure to look for the previous books in
Julie Anne Lindsey's Beaumont Brothers Justice:

Closing In On Clues
Always Watching
Innocent Witness

Available now wherever
Harlequin Intrigue books are sold!